The Vegas Kid

The Vegas Kid

by Barney Vinson

HUNTINGTON PRESS

LAS VEGAS, NEVADA

The Vegas Kid

Published by
    Huntington Press
    3687 South Procyon Avenue
    Las Vegas, Nevada 89103
    (702) 252-0655 Phone
    (702) 252-0675 Fax
    e-mail: books@huntingtonpress.com

ISBN 0-929712-15-3

Cover Design: Laurie Shaw
Interior Design & Production: Laurie Shaw

Acknowledgments

This book took 15 years to write. I started it when I was working as a dice dealer at the old Dunes Hotel in Las Vegas. Life was giving me a few punches in the mid-section; one more hard shot and I might be on the canvas for good. I was going through a divorce, I needed back surgery, the Dunes was about to go under, my income had dried up like a desert creek bed, and I was three months behind on my house payments.

But humor has always played an important role in my life. My dad taught me to laugh when I was small, and for that trait alone I will always be grateful. It's another of life's sad ironies that he never got to see my name on a book cover.

I also owe a debt of gratitude to the following people who believed in me when I was having trouble believing in myself: first and foremost, my wife Debbie, the best friend and partner a guy could hope for; Harry and Midge Rubinson who kept egging me on; Bobby and Sue Young for their encouragement; Deke Castleman who brought these words to life; Anthony Curtis who had the courage (and incredible foresight) to publish this book; Bethany Coffey Rihel of Huntington Press who pushed and pushed to get it published; and David Tarino, my agent and confidante who got me off my butt and made me finish this story.

It isn't the story of my life. It's the story of everyone's life, and how we cope when things just don't go right. And sometimes, if we're lucky, we end up like the hero does in this book. Turn the page and I'll show you what I mean.

Prologue

The stranger in black turned to the driver. "There she is," he said, waving expansively at the city down below.

Sam peered through the glass. Down below, he could see lights of every color twinkling in the distance. After a hundred miles of mesquite and cactus, it looked like the bejeweled necklace of some giant goddess, flung carelessly across the sand.

Sam's arms tingled and his breath came in ragged bursts. This was the place Lady Luck called home, and he was going there to join her. If someone had told him a month ago that he would be heading to Las Vegas in a motorhome with a complete stranger ... why, he would have laughed himself silly.

Then again, a month ago Sam was a television star with a beautiful home in the Hollywood hills, a beautiful sports car in the driveway, and a beautiful wife in the bedroom.

Yeah, well, that was a month ago.

June, 1972

The alarm clock buzzed and Sam Durango didn't move. It buzzed again and he rolled onto his side, pulling the pillow over his head. It buzzed again and his hand shot out, knocking the clock to the floor.

Sam lifted the pillow just enough for one eye to find the glow-in-the-dark clock dial, which read 4:45. Slowly he sat up, then swung his legs over the side of the bed. He reached out to cover up Monica, then remembered she wasn't there. She and her friend Gladys were in Carmel on a shopping trip, and they wouldn't be back until this afternoon. He rubbed his eyes, got to his feet, and slipped on his robe.

He padded down the hallway to the kitchen and poured himself a tall glass of orange juice. He felt fuzzy, unable to get his thoughts straight. It was like having the television on channel two and trying to watch channel three. Everything was slightly out of focus. And no wonder! An empty vodka bottle on the table lay next to his script. Damn, he hadn't even looked at his lines.

After a long shower, he felt a little better. He dressed, then squinted at himself in the full-length mirror, seeing nothing but a blurry reflection. With a sigh, he fumbled for his contact lenses. He hated those things, but he couldn't make western movies wearing a damn pair of horn-rims. Why, they'd laugh him right off the lot. He smiled wistfully, thinking of what Monica usually said when she watched him go through his morning ritual.

"It's a bird, it's a plane, it's Sam Durango!"

His alligator boots needed polishing, but for now he swiped at them with his towel. Then he walked to the phone and called for a cab. His station wagon was in front of the house, out on the long winding driveway, and his sports car was in the garage, but he needed time to go over the script. He couldn't afford to slow things up on the last day of shooting.

Just as he finished his second orange juice, a horn sounded outside. Sam tucked the script under his arm and jogged to a waiting cab through a light drizzle.

"I'll be dogged!" the cab driver exclaimed as Sam let himself in the back seat. "You're Sam Durango, right?"

"Yup," Sam grunted. "Pioneer Studios on Sunset. And take it slow. I've got some reading to catch up on."

"Yes sir, Mister Durango!" the cab driver called, smiling into the rearview mirror. "We don't want to run down any redskins or school marms, right?"

Ignoring the driver, Sam flipped on a light, opened his script, and thumbed to the last scene. There wasn't that much dialogue. All he had to do was walk into the saloon just as the deputy was squaring off against the two gunfighters. Just walk in nice and easy, stop at the far end of the bar where a piece of tape on the floor marked his place, and—

"—your show every week!" the cab driver was yelling above the thump of the windshield wipers. "My wife ain't gonna believe this."

Sam slapped the script shut and groped for his cigarette papers and tobacco pouch. Might as well enjoy the ride.

"I got a brother going to UCLA!" the driver hollered back at Sam. "He wants to be an actor. Even knows how to ride a horse. I don't suppose you could do anything for him? You know, introduce him to the right people? Help him get his foot in the door?"

There went this guy's tip. "Hell," Sam grumbled. "I'm having a hard time keeping my own foot in the door."

The driver nodded. "Yeah, I guess things are tough all over."

Sam leaned forward. "Hey, he's going to college. Tell him to get into something with a real future. Like geology or zoology. Or—uh—scientology."

The driver touched the brakes and the cab rolled to a stop in front of Pioneer Studios. Then he turned in his seat. "I know a lot of people take advantage of celebrities like you, Mister Durango. So I won't insult you by asking you for your autograph."

"That's nice of you," Sam said, opening his door. "How much do I owe you?"

"Fifty-seven dollars."

After sitting through an hour in the make-up chair, Sam greeted everyone on the set. He knew them all, from the script girl right on up to Jay Cohen, whose father built Pioneer Studios back in the early forties. In fact, Jay Cohen was walking toward Sam now.

"Hello, Sam," Cohen said with a nod. "Wrapping it up today, eh?" He offered Sam a limp white hand, then cleared his throat. "Stop by my office after lunch, will you? We need to have a little talk."

Sam watched him walk away, wondering what Cohen had up his sleeve. This was the last show of the year, and Sam wasn't stupid. He knew his show was slipping badly in the ratings and he'd heard the rumors it might not be renewed. But he had a contract, as well as an agent who was supposed to handle things like this.

The trouble was that every time he made one of these television westerns the plot either got a little flimsier or it had been used half a dozen times. The one he was doing now was typical. The grand finale took place in a saloon with a big showdown between the good guys and the bad guys. Some scriptwriter must have stayed up half the night thinking up this one.

"Places everybody," the director called. "And ... action!"

Sam gives the swinging door a push and walks inside. There is a sudden screeching of chairs as the piano player's song stops abruptly. Sam walks to the end of the bar. The two gunfighters stand watching him. One of them is holding the deputy. The other drops his hands slowly to his sides, his six-shooters within easy reach.

"Well, if it ain't the Vegas Kid," he sneers. "We've been waiting for you."

"Let him go," Sam says softly.

"You hear that, Spike? The Kid's giving orders."

"I'm telling you for the last time," Sam says. "Let him go."

"He's going, all right. Straight to Boot Hill!"

With that, the gunfighter goes for his guns. Sam goes for his in the same instant.

"CUT!"

Sam had forgotten to strap on his gun. "Sorry," he said meekly.

The crew broke for lunch. With a dry mouth Sam started down the studio street to Jay Cohen's office in the administration building, which stood over the lot like a concrete mountain. The rain had let up, but the humidity left Sam's clothes damp to the touch by the time he got to Cohen's office on the third floor.

Two secretaries looked up as Sam came through the door. "Hello, Mister Durango," said the one at the closest desk. "Mister Cohen isn't back from lunch yet. Would you like to wait?"

"Yeah, but I'd like to wash up. Is there a men's room or something around here?"

"You can use Mister Cohen's washroom. I'm sure he wouldn't mind."

Sam turned on the light and locked the bathroom door. Then he let out a low whistle. What a layout. Everything was high-lighted in gold: the fixtures, the carpeting, the walls, even the toilet seat. Sam had busted his chops making TV westerns half his life, and Jay Cohen's bathroom was worth more than he was.

All things considered, though, the years had been good to Sam. Well, his eyesight wasn't too good, but contact lenses solved that problem. He still had most of his hair, even if it was turning prematurely gray. He had his own teeth, somewhere underneath fifteen thousand dollars worth of caps. He was still on the slim side, except for a slight paunch, but a couple of workouts at the health club and he would be as good as new.

At the moment, none of that really mattered. Right now the only thing worth thinking about was Jay Cohen, and why this sawed-off little runt wanted to talk to him. Sam was not fond of the man. Sure, he had money and power, but only because he just happened to be born to the right father.

Sam washed his hands and dried them with a gold face towel. Then as he turned to leave, he dropped the towel into the commode. Humming softly, he flushed it.

"Sit down, sit down," Cohen said primly, motioning to a chair in front of his massive desk. Sam stiffly settled into it.

"So ... did you finish filming this morning?"

"Not quite," Sam said evenly. "I've got to get back, so I hope this doesn't take too long."

"No, no, not at all," Cohen said. "I was going to talk to your agent about this, but—what the heck—we're old friends, aren't we?"

Sam didn't answer.

"We're civilized people. No reason why we can't talk to each other in private, without a bunch of strangers hanging on every word."

Sam shook a line of tobacco into a rolling paper.

"I never dreamed you did that in real life," Cohen laughed. "I thought that was just part of your image."

Sam licked the paper and blew on it softly. "Nope," he said, lighting up.

Cohen let out a mechanical chuckle, then cleared his throat. "Sam, how long has your show been on the air?"

"'The Vegas Kid?'"

"Yes."

"Four years."

"And before that?"

"'Cactus Classics.' That ran for six."

Cohen shuffled through a stack of papers on his desk. "I've got some figures here somewhere that I want to show you."

Sam got to his feet and walked to the window, his back to Cohen. Through the glass he looked out at storm clouds sitting low over the soundstages and foothills that had been home for most of his adult life. The studio lot looked like a little toy city, but suddenly it wasn't his anymore. "You're scratching the show," he said quietly, turning to face Cohen.

Cohen turned his hands up. "What else can I do? I'm a businessman, Sam. I can't let my personal feelings get involved."

"I wouldn't expect you to," Sam replied. "After all, I've only given you ten years of my life."

Cohen leaned back in his chair. "If it makes you feel any better, think of all the little kids out there who learned the history of this great country of ours—thanks to people like you."

"Sounds like you've made that speech before."

"I learned it from my father."

"Your father never said anything of the sort," Sam said. "Your father was a brilliant man. He was an artist. It's a tribute to his memory that this studio is still standing."

Cohen's mouth tightened. "I'm not going to get into a personality conflict with you. I can only go by figures, and they show that people are tired of cowboys and Indians. They want something new, something different."

Sam felt a hard knot form in his stomach. "Don't tell me you're giving me until sundown to get out of town."

"I'm paying off your contract. I'm sorry."

Sam dropped his cigarette in Cohen's ashtray without bothering to squash it out. "Tell me, have you ever thought about getting together with your father again?"

"My father's dead," Cohen said blankly.

"I know."

• • •

Sam walked out the studio gate, expecting to have a thousand different thoughts clawing inside his head. Instead, he felt strangely at peace, with a fierce awareness of everything around him. He could feel the city's vibrations. He smelled rain and flowers and food, mixed together in a sweetly nauseous way. He saw six birds in a tight V formation overhead, winging their way toward the mountains in the distance, and from somewhere nearby he heard music. It sounded like a Beatles song.

He walked down the wet sidewalk, swaying to the music, watching the birds until they were specks in the sky. To hell with Jay Cohen. To hell with the studio, and television ratings. The sun suddenly broke through the clouds. It was going to be a beautiful day, and at the moment nothing else mattered.

Then his feet shot out from under him and he fell into the street.

The doctor was wrapping Sam's right arm. "Sorry about your shirt," he said. "I had to cut the sleeve off."

"So I see." Actually, Sam didn't see, at least not that clearly. Somewhere between the ambulance and the hospital he'd lost one of his dad-blamed contact lenses.

"And you'll have to keep that arm in a sling for a couple of days. You can take it off as soon as the swelling goes down."

When the doctor was finished, Sam eased to his feet. "Is there a phone around here I can use?"

"You'll find some pay phones next to the cashier's office."

"Thanks, doc. By the way, would you do me a favor?"

"Sure."

"Would you get some change out of my pants pocket for me? I can't reach it without using my right hand."

The doctor laughed, reaching into his own pocket. "Here's a dime."

"Thanks, I appreciate it."

"Oh, no problem. I'll just add it to your bill."

Sam called Larry Noble, his agent and the husband of Monica's friend Gladys. "Larry? Sam Durango. There's been an accident, and I'm at General Hospital. Could you get over here? I need to talk to you."

"You okay, Sam?" Noble barked into the phone. "You weren't doing one of your own stunts, were you?"

"No, I'm fine."

"Was it Monica? What happened? She was with Gladys, and they were in Gladys's car! Oh my god! I'll be right there!"

"Larry! Larry!" Sam shouted, but it was too late. The phone was dead. Sam shook his head, then laid the receiver back in its cradle. He turned to see a young boy in a wheelchair staring up at him. The boy's face was pale, but his eyes were wide with excitement.

"You're the Vegas Kid," the boy said haltingly.

"Yup," Sam said softly, squatting in front of the boy.

"What happened to your arm?"

"I—er—got bushwhacked."

"I see you on TV every week. Could I get your autograph? And can you sign it to Tim?"

"Well, sure, little fella. 'Course, it's kinda hard for me to sign anything with my writing hand out of commission and all, but I'll try."

"Thanks, Kid. I can show it to my friends and to Doctor Hollis, and they'll know I really met you."

A nurse handed him a pen and paper, and Sam carefully wrote his name with his left hand.

Sam Durango

Sam eased the pistol from his holster. He thumbed the cylinder open and emptied the blank cartridges into his pocket. Then he held the gun out to Tim. "I can't run things one-handed," Sam said. "Take this. From now on, you're my sidekick."

"Gosh. Thanks, Kid!"

The nurse gave Sam a grateful smile as she wheeled Tim away, but he ducked his head. He needed a smoke and a drink.

Sam was walking through the hospital's front door just as Larry Noble pulled up in his car. Noble flooded him with questions, but Sam cut him short. "Larry, the girls weren't in an accident. I was."

A look of relief crossed Noble's face, then he smiled. "Hey, this might be good publicity. What did you do, wrestle with a bear?"

"No."

"Stop a bank robbery?"

"No."

"Catch somebody jumping from a burning building?"

"No."

"Well—what happened?"

"I slipped on the sidewalk."

"You slipped? On the sidewalk? That's what happened?"

"Well, hell, Larry, it was wet. I'm surprised no one else got hurt."

Noble didn't answer, so Sam let the conversation die. He turned awkwardly in the seat and cranked down the window. They drove toward the ocean, the screeching car radio filling the silence. Finally they came to a weathered wooden building with a big sign out front: THE FISH HOUS. The E on the last word had been missing for as long as Sam could remember. It was Noble's favorite restaurant.

"Hungry?" Noble asked, uttering his first word since they left the hospital.

"I could eat something, I guess."

They entered through a small cluttered bar, the smell of stale beer hanging in the air. Two men sat at the counter, and they gave Noble and Sam a short curious look before returning to a rummy argument.

"Let's go outside," Sam said. "I need some peace and quiet."

"Fine."

They took a table by the railing, and a waitress gave them menus. Sam squinted to make out the name tag on her uniform, "Valerie." She was one of those California girls that all the songs had been written about. Sam's blurry gaze flew to her hair, then circled her lips several times before crash landing on her shapely tan legs.

"How's the seafood today?" he asked.

"Fresh," she said, her eyes meeting his.

Though he couldn't see her clearly, she was a looker, no doubt about it. Long blonde hair, full sensuous lips, eyes that were—well, it was kind of hard to tell about the eyes. She wore a huge pair of glasses with red lenses, so he couldn't tell what color they were. Probably blue. Blondes always had blue eyes.

Sam watched her go, then come back with their drinks: a beer for Noble and a double martini on ice for Sam. "This is like my career," Sam said, hoisting the glass. "On the rocks."

Noble lit a wooden-tipped cigar, then he leaned across the table. "So what happened today?"

"I told you already. I slipped on the damn sidewalk."

"No, I mean before that. At the studio."

"Oh, that."

"Jay Cohen called me and he was furious. He said you walked off the set, and now they've got to rewrite the whole ending of the show."

Sam poked at the olive in his glass. "He fired me, you know."

"He paid off your contract. I know all about it. And then you walk off right in the middle of the last day of shooting." Noble shook his head. "I don't know, Sam. Cohen is really pissed. He's talking about filing a complaint with the Screen Actors Guild."

Sam turned toward his agent. "Larry, I've been grinding out that cowboy crap for ten years. I go in today and Cohen gives me the ax. What am I supposed to do, hang around there the rest of my life in case he changes his mind?"

Both men were quiet as Valerie brought food and fresh drinks to the table. Sam watched her walk away again, then Noble broke the silence. "You should have finished that last scene, Sam. That's all I'm saying."

Sam started on his new martini. "Well, the truth is, I forgot. I really did, Larry. Cohen had just fired me. When I walked out of his office, I wasn't thinking straight." After a pause, he added, "And I obviously wasn't *walking* straight."

Noble held up his hand. "The thing you've got to remember is that Jay Cohen is a pretty important person in this town, regardless of how you feel about him personally. At this point in your career, you don't need to make any enemies."

"What makes you think I don't like the asshole?" Sam took a fork in his left hand and tried to cut off a bite of fish. "I don't know what it is about big business nowadays. Some immigrant comes over here, works his butt off to build a multimillion dollar empire out of a pipe dream, then gives it to his son to run into the ground. Sometimes I wish this *was* the old West, and I really was a gunfighter. I'd round up every boss's son in town, and string 'em up by their long skinny necks."

Noble cracked a crab leg, then looked up at Sam. "Oh, so now you want to change the world. Here you are, out of work, your arm in a sling, mud on your pants, an empty holster on your belt. What happened to your gun anyway?"

"I gave it to somebody. I'm not using it anymore."

"Oh Sam, for crying out loud!"

Sam sighed, then set his fork down. He couldn't eat left-handed, and he certainly wasn't going to ask Larry Noble to hand-feed him.

"Sam, you're supposed to be a movie star."

"TV star."

"TV star. And look at you."

Sam looked down, then back at Noble.

"Image," Noble was saying. "It's all image, Sam. You look important, you feel important. Eventually, you'll be important."

"Don't talk to me about important. How am I supposed to look important when I'm always in this damn costume?"

Noble filled his glass with beer and lightly salted it. "I know you don't like Jay Cohen, but he's right about one thing. People are tired of television westerns. Yours was the last one on the air. People want sitcoms now. Look at 'All in the Family.' It's the number one show on the air. And you know why? Because people want to laugh, forget their problems. It's a changing world, Sam."

"I'm willing to change with it, Larry."

"Well, it's not that simple. I'm afraid you're typecast. You've been doing these cowboy shows for so many years that the public won't accept you in any other role, Sam. I suggest you take a little vacation. Relax for a few days. In the meantime, I'll try to line up some work for you. Livestock shows, rodeos, county fairs, things like that."

"Gee, thanks."

Noble exploded. "If you don't like it, then maybe you should find yourself another agent! I mean it! I should be at six different places right now, and what am I doing? I'm sitting here trying to explain the facts of life to some washed-up movie star."

"TV star."

"Whatever. And I'll tell you something else. The only reason I took you on as a client in the first place was because Gladys and Monica were such good friends."

"If you're such a great agent, then how come I'm out of work?"

With a cold stare, Noble rose to his feet. "That's it. You can insult Jay Cohen all you want, but you're not insulting me. I've had it. Find yourself another agent!"

"Larry, wait," Sam said feebly, but Noble had already walked away. He drained his martini and waved for another. He tried to focus on his watch; it was after four. Monica should be home by now, but he wasn't ready to face her. Things were bad enough between them already. He couldn't just walk in and say, "Hi, I lost my job and I walked off the set and I hurt my shoulder and I don't want you running around with Gladys because I just had a fight with her husband and he's not my agent anymore." She'd be at her lawyer's office before he knew what hit him.

Valerie came with his drink. "Thanks," he said.

"What's the matter? You didn't like your meal?"

"I wasn't hungry. How much do I owe you, anyway?"

"Your friend paid for everything before he left."

"Oh."

Valerie turned to leave, then stopped. "By the way, Mister Durango, if you're ever down at the beach, look me up. I'll be at the Devil's Sink Hole Grill."

"That's where you live?"

"No," she laughed. "I'm going to work there."

"You've got two jobs?"

"No, this is my last day here. I can make more money on the beach."

Money! Maybe she was hinting for a tip. Sam turned sideways in his chair, trying to reach the money in his right pocket with his left hand. By the time he got his money out, Valerie was gone. Sam finished his drink and rose unsteadily to his feet. It was time to face the music.

As Sam walked through the bar, he noticed the two men again at the counter. The argument between them was getting louder, and Sam looked around for the bartender. They were just like cops, never around when you needed one. Suddenly, both men were on their feet. One swung at the other and missed. The momentum caused him to stumble, and he went down to his knees. The other man stood over him, his fists cocked.

"Hey!" Sam hollered, getting between them. "Why don't you two just shake hands? Come on, I don't want to see anybody get hurt."

He stretched out his left hand to help the fallen man get to his feet. In doing so, however, he took his eyes off the other man. CRACK! Sam blinked his eyes several times. Stars appeared, thousands and thousands of them, and then they blinked off, one by one.

"Don't wanna see anybody get hurt," he said again. Then he fell to the floor.

Sam opened one eye. It seemed to have rusty hinges on it. He opened the other eye. There was his doctor again. He was talking, but Sam couldn't make out the words.

"Hmm?"

"Howdooyew feel?"

"Head hurts."

"YewsufferedaminorconCUSHion."

"Huh?" To Sam, everything sounded like it was underwater.

"I said, you suffered a minor concussion."

"What happened?"

"Oh, some old codger in a bar out on the Pacific Coast Highway hit you in the head with a beer bottle." Wrinkling his nose, he added, "And apparently it wasn't empty at the time."

Every other word was lost somewhere between Sam's ears and his brain, but he got the gist. "Oh, I remember now," Sam said, sitting up on the table. "There was a fight. I tried to break it up." He gingerly touched the bandage on his head.

"The cashier's office is down the hall."

"Yeah, I remember."

"And here's another dime."

"Hey, it's you! You're the Vegas Kid!"

Sam stopped in the hallway. A nurse was wheeling a small boy toward him.

"How yuh doing, little fella?" Sam tried to smile.

"Not so good," the little boy answered. Then the words came tumbling out. "You know Tim Bartlett? He's in the hospital with me. There's about twenty of us in the ward. And he said—he said you made him your sidekick. And he's got your gun to prove it. Now he's going around giving everybody orders. How come you made him your sidekick, Kid?"

"What's your name, son?"

"Harold. But everybody calls me Corky."

Sam dug the blank cartridges out of his pocket with his left hand, then held them out to the boy. "Tim's got my gun, Corky, but he doesn't have any bullets. You've got 'em."

Corky held the bullets in his hand like rare jewels. "Gosh."

"He can't very well shoot anybody without your help. So you two are gonna have to work in cahoots from now on."

"Gee, thanks, Kid!"

"But you should use them only on special occasions, like the Fourth of July. What do you think, nurse?"

The nurse shot him a dirty look. "A wonderful idea. Here, Corky. I'll keep those bullets in a safe place for you," and she practically ripped them out of his hand.

Sam watched them go, then managed to get the dime into the pay phone. After two rings, Monica answered.

"Sam, where are you?"

"I'm at the hospit—" He stopped. There was no use going into all that right now. "I'm downtown. I don't have my car."

"I know."

"Well, how about picking me up?"

No answer.

"If it's too much trouble, I can grab a cab."

No answer.

"So that's what I'll do. I'll just get a cab and I'll—"

"Sam, what happened today? Gladys just called and said that you and Larry had some kind of big blowup. She said that Larry said that you said that—oh, I don't know. None of it made any sense."

"Everything's fine," Sam tried to reassure her, even though

his head was buzzing and one eye was blurry. "I'll see you when I get home."

"Where are you?"

"I'm at the hospit—I'm downtown. On Hollywood Boulevard. Why don't you pick me up and we'll go somewhere for dinner. Anywhere you want."

"Well, I didn't fix anything for dinner. Why don't we go to the Breakers? I'm dying for some fresh seafood."

Sam's stomach suddenly shifted. "How about if we pick up a pizza?"

"Sam, I want seafood."

"Okay, we'll have 'em put anchovies on it."

Sam strolled aimlessly down the boulevard, oblivious to the light rain that was falling again. His arm was starting to ache and his head was still throbbing. Maybe a good night's sleep and he'd be good as new. He looked down idly at the bronze stars embedded in the sidewalk, one of Hollywood's last-ditch efforts to regain its faded splendor. Stopping in front of one to read the inscription, he was almost knocked off-balance as a woman bumped into him from behind. She cried out as her grocery bag spilled to the ground.

The woman, dressed in black, had gray hair and wore shoes with squatty wooden heels and an old-fashioned pair of wire-rimmed spectacles. She reminded Sam of his Aunt Lucy, who lived in Texas and grew apricot trees in her backyard.

Sam hunched down and began gathering the spilled groceries as the woman chased a grapefruit bouncing down the sidewalk. Sam dropped half a dozen oranges into the bag and started to pick up a sticky seed-splattered cantaloupe. Looking around to make sure the woman was not watching, he kicked her cantaloupe into the gutter.

By now everything else was back in the bag except for a small box of chocolate cookies at Sam's feet. "Here," he said, smiling at her. "Let me help you get your cookies."

She snatched her bag, and hurried away. "Pervert!"

Sam shook his head sadly. Larry Noble was right about

one thing. It *was* a changing world. He started down the side-walk again, stopping again to read the next bronze star. "GENE AUTRY."

Stepping on the star with his boot, he said, "Here, Gene. Have some filet of sole."

Farther down the block he paused in front of an appliance store with a display of television sets inside the window. A different picture flickered on each: a newscaster, an "I Love Lucy" episode, a cartoon, a baseball game. But the one that caught Sam's attention was the big set in the middle. It showed a strange-looking fellow in an outlandish costume. The man wore a western outfit with one sleeve cut off. Some kind of orange seedy stuff covered one of the man's boots, and there were black smears on his pants legs. One arm was in a sling, his head was wrapped in a white bandage that resembled a turban, and on the man's waist was some kind of leather apparatus. Sam pointed at the man. The man pointed back at Sam. "Oh no," he whispered, realizing with dull panic that he was watching himself on a closed-circuit television.

He turned toward the street and wiped his boots on the back of his pants legs. Then he held out his hand to see if the rain had stopped. At that moment a well-dressed couple walked past. The woman saw Sam and nudged her companion. "Honey," she said quietly.

"Okay, okay," the man mumbled, reaching into his pocket. He dropped a quarter in Sam's outstretched hand. "Here you go, buddy," he said. Then he whispered, "Get a job."

Monica drove by slowly in the station wagon. She passed Sam and kept going. Halfway down the block the car pulled over to the curb. Sam walked as fast as he could without jiggling his arm too much. He stood by the side of the car, trying to open the passenger door with his left hand. Finally, Monica leaned over and opened it for him.

He settled into the seat while Monica studied him quietly. As she pulled back into traffic she asked, "Do you want to stop for a pizza? Or would you prefer to go through an automatic car wash first?"

"Oh, you mean this?" Sam asked, touching his shoulder, then his head, then his empty holster.

"You told me on the phone that everything was fine."

"I said everything was going to *be* fine."

"You said everything *was* fine."

"What if I did?"

"Well, it obviously isn't fine!"

Monica blasted her horn as she roared past a school bus, stopped and red lights flashing, then shot an angry look at Sam. "My mother tried to tell me but I wouldn't listen."

Sam looked glumly out the window. "Hey, up at the corner. A pizza shop. Pull in."

"Our whole world is falling apart, and you want a pizza."

"I'm not even hungry. I don't care if I never see food again, and I mean it."

She smiled. "In that case, let's eat."

Monica stopped the car. "I think it would be best if I got the pizza," she said, her eyes straight ahead. Sam leaned forward and got out his wallet with his left hand. "You smell like a brewery," she said, grabbing the wallet.

"I tried to stop a fight and this old guy clobbered me with a beer bottle."

"So you hit him and broke your arm?"

"I slipped on a wet sidewalk. It could've happened to anyone."

"And your toy gun went flying off into the wild blue yonder?"

"I gave it to a little boy in the hospital."

"Oh, Jesus, Sam." She got out of the car, gave him one last glare, then slammed the door.

Soon they were back on the highway. Monica held a wedge of pizza in one hand as she drove. "Come on, Sam, eat something," she said, glancing over at him.

"I'll wait till we get home," he said. "I want to get out of these clothes first. Then have a leisurely drink. And then take a nice long bath. And then—"

"Do you hear something?" Monica interrupted.

"What?"

"Listen."

Ker BLAP, ker BLAP, ker BLAPPETY BLAP. Ker BLAPPETY FLAPPETY BLAPPETY FLAP. It sounded like a Beatles song.

"Pull over!" Sam shouted. "I think you've got a flat tire!"

"I've got a flat tire? You mean, we've got a flat tire!"

Sam poked his head out the window. "Yup, we've got a flat tire." He turned sideways in the seat and pushed the door open. Then he walked to the back of the station wagon. "Monica!" he called. "Where's the spare?"

"What?"

Sam walked back to the passenger door and leaned in. "Where's the spare?"

"In the garage."

"Our garage?"

"Yes."

"Well, what's it doing there?"

"There's more room in the garage."

Sam slowly climbed back into the car. A minute went by, and then another. The only sound was cars whizzing past on the highway.

"Sam, what are we going to do?"

He let out a long slow sigh. "Take the flat tire off, roll it to a service station, get it fixed, roll it back, put it on, and SELL THIS GODDAMN STATION WAGON!"

"You don't have to shout at me," she said patiently. "I'm sitting right here."

"I'M SORRY!"

"Now if you honestly feel that the tire has to be taken off and changed, then go ahead and do it. I'll wait here."

"Uh, yeah, okay. Put the emergency flasher on. Just in case."

She pulled the flasher knob and a puff of smoke wafted

out of the dashboard. "That's funny," she frowned. "That never happened before."

Sam shook his head and walked to the rear of the car. He pulled the jack out of the trunk and knelt next to the flat tire. Then he fitted the lug wrench over one of the wheel nuts and tried to turn it with his left hand. It wouldn't budge. He tried again, straining every muscle in his body. The damn things were welded on.

He walked back to the passenger door. "What's the matter now?" she asked, looking up.

"The nuts won't come off."

"The what?"

"The—things holding the tire on. They're stuck. They won't come off."

She opened her door. "Let me try," she said. Sam practically bit his lip to keep from laughing. Here was Monica in a powdery blue dress and high-heels, her hair done up in delicate swirls, and she—

Zip. Zip, zip, zip. Zip, zip.

"Now what?" she asked, handing Sam the lug wrench and the six nuts. He scratched his head, then jacked up the car, hoisted off the tire, and let it flop on the ground. "Well, I guess I'll be rolling along."

"All right, Sam."

"It might take me awhile. Why don't you try to flag down a cab, and I'll see you back at the house."

"Well, it is getting dark."

He reached for the tire.

"Sam, are you sure you're all right?"

"I'm fine. I've never felt better in my life. By the way, you don't have any really strong pain pills in your purse, do you?"

Sam rolled the flat tire down the side of the road. It was raining again. He was thirsty. The pain in his right shoulder was getting worse, and so was his headache. Even worse, he had to take a whiz, and there was not one damn tree in sight. This was supposed to be California?

Up ahead he saw a billboard. He stopped but the tire didn't; it rolled toward the ditch. Sam let it go, looking up at the sign. The words were big enough for him to read, even with one contact lens.

WILD WEST COUNTRY HOEDOWN
STARRING
* * * BUCK BEAUMONT * * *
AND HIS WONDER DOG BLUE JAY
WHITEY'S CASINO
LAS VEGAS
OCT 27 - OCT 30

The rugged face of Buck Beaumont stared stoically ahead like one of the presidents on Mount Rushmore. "Hey, Buck!" Sam hollered. "You're looking good for an old fart."

Sam waited for a lull in the traffic, then unzipped his trousers with his left hand. He was thinking about Buck Beaumont and his wonder dog Blue Jay. He knew them both, and the idea of Blue Jay being a "wonder dog" almost made Sam laugh as he relieved himself on the side of the road.

Blue Jay was half-Chihuahua and half-Pekingese and mean

as a half-crazed grizzly. Blue Jay hated anything that was bigger than he was, which included Buck Beaumont and Sam Durango. Every time Sam dropped by Buck's house, Blue Jay nipped at his boot heels from the moment he arrived until the moment he left.

The only way Buck could even get close to Blue Jay in one of their western shows was by hiding beef jerky in his pockets. If Blue Jay were ever examined by the S.P.C.A., countless scars would be found where people had kicked and thrown things at him while trying to protect their lives and loved ones.

Then there was Virginia, the black-haired beauty Buck had married when she was barely out of high school. They were divorced two years later and she just disappeared. Even the *National Enquirer* couldn't find her. Sam felt a twinge of guilt thinking about her. In a way their divorce was his fault.

He'd been invited to dinner one night when Monica was out of town. Buck wasn't home from the studio yet and Virginia was in the kitchen cooking tacos. She got something in her eye and Sam was close to her, trying to help, when Buck walked in.

"Don't ever touch my wife again!" he roared at Sam.

Sam backed away, not knowing what to say. It was like a scene from an old movie, and Sam kept waiting for the director to holler, "Cut!" Then he heard a yelp. He was standing on Blue Jay's tail.

"And don't ever touch my dog again, either."

Sam and Buck were good friends, though, back in the beginning. Buck worked on a dude ranch in Wyoming, then moved to California to break into the movies. They met at Frontier Studios, where both of them were cast as ranch hands in a picture called *Guns Across the Colorado*. Money was tight and Sam was having trouble paying the rent on his small beach bungalow. When he learned that Buck was staying at the Y.M.C.A., Sam invited him to move in.

It turned out Buck was a great poker player. He could play anything: five-card draw, seven-card stud, Texas hold 'em.

When he sat at a poker table, Buck's whole personality changed. He was like a machine, rumbling along in neutral until that one magical hand came along, then he'd put it all on the line. Afterwards, he'd come through the door of the beach house, enough money in hand to pay the rent for another thirty days.

He and Buck kept cranking out "B" movies at the studio, though their names never appeared in the credits. They were Confederate soldiers in *Hands Across the Rio Grande*, fur traders in *Drums Across the Mississippi*, Indian scouts in *Peacepipes Across the Potomac*.

It was about this time that Sam left Frontier Studios to go to Pioneer Pictures, where Jay's father, Morris Cohen, signed him for the lead in "Cactus Classics." Old Moe believed in realism, and "Cactus Classics" was filmed every week in an authentic western town constructed for the show in the San Fernando Valley. Real cowboys and Indians were used whenever possible, and even though he was the star, Sam remembered doing three shows in a row without a single line of dialogue.

Meanwhile, Buck wound up doing bit parts at Frontier for the next two years. By then, Sam lived in a sprawling house in the hills and was a man about town. He tried to help Buck, even getting him a starring role on one of the episodes of "Cactus Classics." In fact, Buck used a film clip of that segment to get an audition at Cavalier Studios, where he eventually landed the lead in the television series "Sagebrush Stories."

On the day Buck signed his contract, Sam bought him a big yellow Cadillac convertible. The car was Sam's way of saying "congratulations" and "good luck" and "sorry about the divorce" and everything else he couldn't put into words. Buck barely thanked him.

Maybe it was because Sam made the big time first. Maybe it was because by then, Sam was happily married to Monica, the Playmate of the Month in October of 1964, and Buck was still living alone in their former digs. That was when Sam began to understand Buck's resentment for him.

Sharing a house on the beach might have been a mistake, but at the time it was a matter of necessity. Of course, a man never really knows another man until they live under the same roof, and in Buck Beaumont's case that was an understatement.

Buck would wear the same pair of socks until they got toe-holes in them, then wear them backwards. The rest of his clothes lay where he dropped them, all over the bungalow. Whenever Sam entertained, he would push Buck's things into a corner with a long stick and cover the mess with a beach towel.

Buck would get Sam's newspaper when it came in the morning, then disappear into the bathroom with it. He always turned straight to the personals in the classified section, and Sam could hear him chuckling through the thin wooden door, hour after agonizing hour.

The crowning blow came one day around lunchtime when Sam was brushing his teeth. Buck watched him rinse his mouth, then said, "You through with that toothbrush yet?" No wonder Virginia left him.

It was a shame their marriage didn't work out, because Sam genuinely liked Virginia. She was a pretty thing, with jet black hair and crystal blue eyes the size of silver dollars. She was short, and Sam liked that in a girl. It made him feel more masculine, more sure of himself when he was around her.

With a sigh, Sam turned away from the billboard. No use thinking about Buck Beaumont and his wonder dog and his busted marriage. It was getting dark, and time for him to get that tire fixed. He walked back to the road, craning his head to look for lights in the distance. Surely there was a service station or a garage around here somewhere.

At that moment a battered old Chevrolet rolled off the highway and came to a wheezy stop next to him. The hood was purple, the front fender was green, and the rest of the car was rust-colored. A ragged Mexican flag hung limply from the radio aerial, and on the hood was a glittering chrome ornament of an eagle with its wings spread.

A young man in the front seat rolled down the passenger window. "Hey, you want a ride, man?"

Sam walked closer to the car, peering inside. Three men sat in the car, two in the front, one in the back, all of whom appeared to be in their early twenties. Their hair was black and greasy, and they wore identical jackets with some kind of emblem on them.

"My car had a flat," Sam said slowly. "I've been looking for a service station."

"Yeah, well, the gas station is a few miles ahead. Hop in. We'll give you a ride."

"Okay." What the hell, Sam could walk down this road until February. "Let me get my tire. It's over here, in the ditch."

"Okay, man." The driver raced his engine several times, then turned it off. The car backfired and Sam quickly checked himself for bullet holes. Then he edged down into the ditch, where he immediately sank to his ankles in mud. Letting out a string of curses, he finally got a grip on the tire and rolled it to the car.

"Madre de Dios," said the guy in the back seat.

"I'm sorry," Sam gasped. "You guys got a blanket or anything? Or I could just hang on your hood ornament if you drive real slow."

The driver of the car hopped out. "Let me check in the trunk."

He unlocked the trunk and kicked at it with a shiny boot. It slowly wobbled open, and to Sam it was like looking into a display window at Macy's. There were eight-track tape decks, Polaroid cameras, transistor radios, calculators, an electric toaster, several men's suits, and two large plastic bags filled with what appeared to be dried grass.

"You need anything, man?" the driver called over to Sam.

"No, thanks."

"How about a suit? You look like you could use some real clothes, man."

"Uh, how much are they?"

"Five dollars."

"No, I don't think so. But thanks anyway."

"How about some good weed, man? It's heavy duty. I can let you have a lid for—fifteen dollars."

Fifteen dollars? He could buy three suits for that. "Thanks, no," he said hastily.

"Okay, man." The driver pulled out an electric blanket that was still in its original wrapper. He tore off the plastic and spread the blanket over the rest of the things in the trunk. "Throw your tire on this. And your boots, too, man."

After a painful struggle, Sam finally got his boots off, then squished to the passenger door in his wet socks. He climbed into the back seat, and the car rumbled onto the highway. "What's your name?" the driver asked, fiddling with the radio. A sudden blare of mariachi music drowned out Sam's reply.

"My name is José!" the driver shouted.

"José? Howdy!"

The man in the front passenger seat turned. "My name is Francisco!" he hollered.

"Francisco? Howdy!"

The man next to Sam grinned, and two gold teeth illuminated the car with a shaft of light. "My name is Pepe," he said.

Sam's ears were still ringing. "Pee Pee? Howdy!"

Pepe thumped José on the shoulder. "Hey, man, this dude called me Pee Pee." José and Francisco laughed, while Pepe continued to grin at Sam. "Pepe, man. No Pee Pee. Pepe."

"Sorry," Sam shrugged, rubbing his ears. "I never could get the hang of español. I can say la cucaracha, but that's about it. My dad used to call me that."

"That's a cockroach, man," Pepe grinned. Then his face grew serious. "Hey, were you in some kind a accident? I don't want to hurt your feelings, man, but you look terrible. You don't smell too good, either. Ai, chihuahua."

"Actually, I lost my footing on a sidewalk and I— " Oh, what was the use? It was just too complicated to explain. Sam fumbled out his cigarette papers and tobacco pouch, and began to laboriously roll a smoke with his left hand. Pepe thumped Francisco on the shoulder. Francisco nudged José. José turned, and his face lit up.

"Hey, man, don't be greedy. Send that baby to papa." He sucked greedily on Sam's hand-rolled cigarette. "WOOH! A-number-one dynamite," he exploded, filling the car with smoke.

Francisco was next. He inhaled, and instantly half of the cigarette disappeared.

"Come on, cabrón," Pepe grinned. "Save some for me, man."

Sam decided that further conversation was useless and settled back into his seat. Suddenly something thumped him. Cautiously, he turned in his seat. It was one of those imitation dogs with a head that nodded up and down with the motion of the car. Sam's attention wasn't on the dog, however, but on the red flashing lights he saw through the rear window.

"Excuse me, fellas. There's a police car behind us. I think he wants us to stop."

By now the cruiser had pulled alongside them, and the beam of a spotlight was trained on Sam's face. José stepped on the brake and the car bounced to a stop. Sam heard his flat tire banging around in the trunk.

Then his door was yanked open and he found himself looking into the face of the biggest highway patrolman he had ever seen. "Yes, officer? What can I do for you?" Sam asked.

"Gonna have to ask you to git out of the car."

"Yes, certainly, officer." Sam slowly climbed out of the back seat, feeling the small rocks on the roadway through his wet socks. "I don't even know these Latin American gentlemen, officer. They were kind enough to offer me a ride. You see, I had a flat tire, and they were taking me to a service station to get it fixed. So —if you'll just give me my tire—and my boots— I'll be on my way."

"Hold it, buddy." The highway patrolman was looking at

Sam's bandage, the sling on his arm, then finally settling on his empty holster.

"Officer, I'll be happy to explain. You see, I'm a—"

"Arrest this one, too, Dave. Suspicion of armed robbery."

"Armed robbery? But that's ridiculous."

The patrolman's hands were going lightly over Sam's clothing. He stopped and stuck a hand in Sam's pocket, retrieving his cigarette papers and tobacco pouch.

"And possession of a controlled substance!"

Sam heard voices and opened his eyes. He was lying on a narrow cot and there were bars on the door. At first he thought he was having a bad dream, but then the memories filtered back. Sam Durango, star of "Cactus Classics" and "The Vegas Kid," was in the pokey!

His watch read two-thirty. He glanced around the cell and saw two men, their hands grasping the bars.

"It's all yo fault, muhfugger."

"Who you callin muhfugger, cogsugger?"

"Who you callin cogsugger, fart blossom?"

"Who you callin fart blossom, ass eyes?"

"Who you callin ass eyes, butt breath?"

"Who you callin—"

"HEY!" Sam hollered.

"'Scuse me?" Both men turned to face him.

"What time is it?" Sam groaned.

One of the men peered at his watch, then announced, "It's two ... thirty ... two."

"Is that morning or afternoon?"

The man chuckled. "Lawd have mercy on a crutch. Must've been some party, my man."

The other man, wearing a uniform with "Leroy" sewn over the shirt pocket, joined in. "Pee yem, my man. Pee yem."

The first man looked at Sam and said, "And in yo case, dat stand for post mortem!"

Suddenly keys clanged at the cell door. "Durango?" a guard barked. "Sergeant says you can make a phone call if you want."

Sam got out of the bunk and hobbled to the door in his socks. Then he followed the guard to a small green room that smelled of stale coffee and Ajax. A table off to the side had a phone on it. Sam opened his wallet and sorted through it. He found his lawyer's business card, dialed a number, and waited.

"Hughes, Watts, Wynn, Weir, and Howe," a chirpy voice answered.

"Stephen Howe, please."

Sam waited for a few moments.

"This is Stephen Howe."

"Mister Howe? This is Sam Durango."

"Yes?"

"I'm in jail."

"Where?"

"I don't know. Downtown somewhere."

"Why?"

"I don't know. Apparently someone thinks I stole something."

"When?"

"Last night."

"How?"

"How?"

"Yes, how?" Howe said.

"I dunno. Just get me out of here, will yuh?"

"Now?"

Sam slammed the phone down.

The guard took him to another room. Two detectives eyed Sam quietly as he came in. The guns on their belts were real ones. One of them motioned Sam to a chair and brought him a pen and paper. "Sign this release and you're free to go. Everything's been cleared up as far as you're concerned."

Sam scrawled his name across the bottom of the page with his left hand.

"What about my tire?" he asked. "It was in—uh—José's trunk. And my boots."

"Need 'em for evidence."

"*You* need them? What about *me*? I've got no shoes. My car is on the side of some freeway with a flat tire and no spare. I haven't been home in two days and my wife's gotta be worried sick. Come on, fellas, give me a break."

The detective nodded to his partner. "Get his stuff, Al." Then he looked back at Sam. "Anybody ever tell you that you look a little like Sam Durango, the movie star?"

"TV star."

"TV star."

Sam rolled the flat tire down the steps of the police station, half-blinded by the afternoon sun. He caught sight of his attorney. Propping the tire against a parking meter, he extended his left hand. "Mister Howe? Thanks for getting down here so quick."

Howe cautiously shook hands with him, looking from the bandage to the sling to the tire.

"Sorry," Sam said. "We can put that in your trunk. Do you have a blanket, or anything?"

They dropped the tire off at a service station. There was a small cafe across the street, and Sam headed for it with the instinct of a wild animal trying to get to its lair before winter sets in. There was coffee in there, hot black coffee, and long tall Bloody Marys.

Howe toyed with his tie while they waited for their food. "Mister Durango, I don't know how to tell you this, but your wife's lawyer called this morning. She wants a divorce."

"A divorce?" Sam echoed, his heart thumping.

"Yes, she's quite upset. The first thing she saw when she woke up this morning was a story about you in the newspaper."

"Uh oh."

"Apparently some reporter found out about you getting arrested. It wasn't a big article, so hopefully not too many people saw it. It was back on the obituary page."

"That figures."

"And then one of your wife's friends called and told her that you'd lost your job at Pioneer Pictures and severed your business relationship with your agent. She's quite upset," Howe repeated.

"Well, maybe I can straighten it all out when I get home."

"I don't think so, Mister Durango. She's already signed a restraining order against you, so I'll have to ask you for your house key."

Sam glumly pried the key from his key ring with his left hand and slid it across the table.

"The only thing we have to do now is work out some sort of financial settlement," Howe said.

Sam bit his lip. "What are you going to do, dissect me right here in public like a dead bullfrog?"

"It isn't as bad as all that," Howe chuckled dryly. He reached into his pocket and dropped a check on the table. It read: "Pay to the order of Sam Durango the sum of $20,000 and no/100."

"What's this?" he asked, giving Howe a hard stare.

Howe smoothed his hair back. "That's the payoff on your contract with Pioneer Studios."

Sam groped for his cigarette fixings. Damn, the cops had taken his tobacco pouch. "Look, Mister Howe. It doesn't take a financial genius to figure this out. I'm supposed to be getting eight hundred thousand dollars a year. Twenty from eight hundred leaves seven hundred and eighty. Where's the rest of it?"

Howe smoothed his hair again. "Well, there's living expenses for your wife, of course. She's got to live, too. Then there's federal withholding taxes, state withholding, Social Security, Medicare, Medicaid, hospitalization insurance, union dues, pension plan, your agent's commission, and of course a small fee for Hughes, Watts, Wynn, Weir, and Howe."

He shrugged and gave Sam a sympathetic look. "You won't be left destitute, Mister Durango. Your wife wants you to have the station wagon, and the twenty thousand dollars of course, and another twenty thousand on the first of the year. She will also give you an additional forty thousand dollars in exchange for the house, the vacant lot behind it, and the sports car, and the furniture, and her jewelry, and the artwork, and the stocks and bonds. Oh, and the little bitty piece of property in Palm Springs."

"You mean the little bitty piece of property in downtown Palm Springs," Sam said bitterly.

"I'm sorry, Mister Durango. I'm just an intermediary."

Intermediary? Muhfuggin' cogsuggin' butt breath thieving lawyer was more like it. "Tell me," he said suddenly. "If the shoe was on the other foot, what would you do?"

"I would give her what she wanted. After all, she's being represented by one of the best lawyers in town."

"Yeah, and who's that?"

"Lyle E. Mortimer. He's the one who handled my wife's first divorce."

Howe dropped Sam and his tire off at the station wagon, giving him a cheery wave as he drove away. Sam didn't wave back. He was trying to figure out what it was about his car that didn't look right. Walking closer, he saw that the jack was missing. Some dirty sidewinder must have stolen it, or else the cops had it down at the police station.

Something else was wrong. The station wagon appeared closer to the ground than he remembered. What the hell? His other three tires were gone! With a sigh, he hitched up his pants and started down the road. Up ahead he saw Buck's billboard.

"Screw you, Buck Beaumont," he said, taking a long step.

"Screw you, Blue Jay," he said, taking another step.

"Screw you, Monica," and another step.

"Screw you, Gladys."

"Screw you, Larry."

"Screw you, Cohen."

"Screw you, Hughes."

"Watts."

"Wynn."

"Weir."

"Howe."

"José."

"Francisco."

"Pee Pee."

His only friend in the whole world seemed to be that waitress at the restaurant where he and Larry had their big fight. What was her name again? Vivian? No ... Oh, yeah. Valerie!

"Need a lift?"

An old Chrysler rolled to a stop.

"Screw you, too!" Sam cried, backing away from the car. The bandage on his head unwound and trailed along behind him.

"What's wrong with that guy?" the driver asked his wife.

"Beats me."

The driver put the car in gear. "Well, let's get home. 'The Vegas Kid' is on TV tonight and I want to watch it. It's one of the last shows of the season."

It was almost five o'clock before Sam got the station wagon back on the road. A tow truck had finally arrived, and three new tires were put on the car. Now here he was behind the steering wheel, knowing things couldn't get any worse ...

WHOOSSH.

Steam was billowing up from underneath the hood, splattering the windshield with dirty water, and the temperature gauge on the dashboard was way over in the red zone. Sam pulled off the road. "Thanks, Monica," he grumbled. "Thanks a lot."

He crawled out of the car and looked around him. The area was completely deserted, except for a long brick building across the road and a sign that read "Curly's." A row of motorhomes was parked in front of it.

Sam felt in his pocket. What the hell, he had twenty thousand dollars, and a station wagon that was clearly on its last legs. With a motorhome, he would at least have a roof over his head. He may have been a cowboy on television, but he'd be damned if he would sleep under the stars.

He got to the building just as a baldheaded man came out the front door. "Can I help you?"

"Yes, I'd like to see Curly."

"I'm Curly."

"Oh. Well, I want to look at some of your motorhomes."

Curly's eyes went from Sam's unraveling bandage to his sling to his muddy boots. "What kind of money are we talking about?"

"Oh, around fifteen thousand cash."

"Yes sir!" he cried, taking Sam by the left arm. "Right this way. And watch your step, sir. Watch your step."

Sam found a motorhome he liked right away. It was literally a little house on wheels. A nice big bed perched over the driver's compartment and there were curtains on the windows. It also had a stove, a sink, and a fold-up dinette. In the back was a small bathroom with a toilet and a small shower.

"Isn't she beautiful?" Curly asked, rubbing his hands together.

"How much?"

It all came out in one breath. "For you seventeen thousand and a three-year or thirty-thousand-mile warranty on everything except parts and labor good at any motorhome repair center inside the continental United States."

Sam shook his head. "I'll give you twelve-five and throw in my station wagon."

"Station wagon? What station wagon?"

"It's over there, on the other side of the road."

"Where? I don't see any station wagon."

"You see that white smoke?"

"Yeah."

"Directly behind that white smoke."

Sam limped after Curly to the station wagon. Curly looked at it sadly. "Now you see, cars just ain't no good anymore. They make the darn things out of tin foil. They last till they're paid for, then you gotta get another one."

Sam couldn't argue with him.

"Why, if I was to rear back and kick the side of your car, it'd probably crumple up like an empty cigarette pack."

"That's okay. I believe you."

Sam followed Curly back to the lot. "Now this here beauty is made out of what you call your fiberglass. It won't dent, no matter what you do."

"It's nice, all right."

"And you can drive it off the lot right now for seventeen thousand."

"I already told you. I'll give you—"

"Sixteen-five."

"Thirteen."

"Sixteen."

"Thirteen-five."

"Fifteen-five."

"Fourteen."

"Fifteen."

"Fourteen."

"Fourteen."

After filling out the necessary papers, Sam climbed into the motorhome and slowly backed out of the lot. Curly came after him, holding something in the air.

"You want this? You left it in your car."

It was Monica's pizza box.

The sun was slipping behind the mountains as Sam drove down the freeway in his new motorhome. A light breeze off the ocean made the palm trees sway and a heavy smell of blossoms filled the air. Down the side of the freeway stretched a sea of purple and white flowers, and up in Hollywood hills lights were flickering. It was the time of day Sam loved best, that gentle easy time between twilight and darkness.

He leaned back in the driver's seat, listening to the hum of rubber on concrete. He remembered when he was growing up in a Texas farm town. Some kids wanted to be doctors. Others wanted to be air force pilots or race car drivers. Not Sam. All he ever wanted was to live in California. He didn't care what he did for a living, as long as he could do it in California.

"You know what California means, don't you?" his dad once asked him. "It's a Spanish word, like cucaracha. It means hot furnace." Sam thought he was kidding.

Ten years later, Sam finally went to California. He felt like he was driving down the road to heaven, especially when he saw the little sign:

CALIFORNIA STATE LINE

He expected to see orange groves and booming surf, maybe a film crew shooting a movie on the side of the road. What a disappointment. All he saw was sand. Not only that, but he arrived in the middle of July. His car didn't have air conditioning, and he drove all the way to Los Angeles with his shirt off and his butt glued to the seat. His father wasn't putting him on after all.

It was worth it, though, when he got to Hollywood and saw the name of the film community hanging in big block letters off a grass-covered hilltop. He didn't even bother getting a room right away. There were too many other things to do.

He went to Schwab's Drug Store, where Lana Turner was discovered. He sat on a red plastic stool, maybe *her* stool, drinking a cherry phosphate out of a glass, maybe *her* glass.

He went to Grauman's Chinese Theater and walked among the hand prints and footprints of all his favorite movie stars.

He stood where John Wayne stood, and for a moment in time he was John Wayne.

He took a Hollywood tour bus past the homes of many show-business legends. He saw Pickfair, the stately mansion built by Mary Pickford and Douglas Fairbanks. He saw Falcon's Lair, the house built by Rudolph Valentino. He saw Lucille Ball's house, and Frank Sinatra's house, and some of Doris Day's dogs romping in the front yard.

Then one night he went into a tiny coffee shop on Vine Street downtown. Sitting at a table less than five feet away was William Holden. Sam almost asked him for his autograph, but then he changed his mind. If he did that, he would come across as a tourist, and that would never do. He wasn't a tourist. He lived in California now, just like William Holden.

Sam's smile turned into a frown as he pulled the motorhome onto the street where he and Monica lived. Or rather, where he and Monica used to live. Or rather, where Monica now lived and he didn't. No lights were on inside, which meant that she probably wasn't home. Now just how was he supposed to get his things?

He walked slowly to the door and rang the bell. No answer. He picked his way around to the rear of the house. Maybe the back door was unlocked. Damn it, he should have brought a flashlight. He couldn't see a thing.

The swimming pool light would help. He flipped the switch, and an eerie glow rose from the pool. The color wasn't blue-green, like it should have been. It was red, and orange, and yellow, and pink, and striped, and polka-dotted. It was the biggest mess Sam had ever seen.

"What the hell?" he muttered, walking over to the edge of the pool.

Damn it! Those were his *clothes* in there!

6

Sam collected his clothes and stumbled back to the motorhome. Dumping the sodden mass inside the shower, he took one last look at his house, the work of a lifetime and the symbol of his success. Then he angrily brushed at a tear and turned away.

The motorhome rumbled down the highway, and on the open road Sam began to feel better. "I'm an old cowhand," he sang, "from the Reee-yo Grande. Dah de um dah doe, dah de um dee DEEE ..."

A sign loomed ahead, pointing the way to the beach. Sam frowned. Somewhere in the back of his mind was a hazy recollection about the beach, something about Satan's Sink or Hell's Kitchen. Well, he didn't have anywhere else to go. He slowed the motorhome and turned off the main highway.

Ah, what a life. In a way, Monica and Jay Cohen and Larry Noble did him a big favor. He was free as a bird now. He could go anywhere under the sun and do anything in the world. He could just flap his wings and take off. How many other people could do that? Heck, he didn't even have to worry about a job, at least for awhile. He would have to put himself on a budget, but he'd get by.

Sam's mind worked. He had six thousand dollars left, the five thousand dollar cashier's check and a thousand dollars in cash that Curly gave him. He was getting twenty thousand next January, and Monica owed him another forty thousand.

That came to sixty-six thousand dollars, and his motorhome was already paid for. It wasn't a fortune by any means, but it beat banging heads with Monica and watching all the money go to a bunch of shyster lawyers.

The beach was closer now. Sam could smell salt air and see the darkness of the ocean off beyond the twinkling lights of the city. What he should do first was find a laundromat and dry out his clothes. Then he could burn the things he was wearing. The Salvation Army wouldn't even take this stuff.

It was late by the time Sam did his laundry, figured out how to light the hot-water heater, took a shower, and got dressed in jeans, a T-shirt, and loafers. He put his arm back in the sling. The shower had eased the pain, but he didn't want to take any chances. As for the bandage on his head, that went into the garbage can along with his cowboy costume. There was just a little cut over his left ear, and it didn't show if he combed his hair straight down on that side. Finally, he climbed into the driver's seat and started the motorhome. He would find a nice restaurant and start thinking things through.

The beach area was deserted. Sam pulled the motorhome to the side of a narrow street, taking up two parking spaces. He walked half a block, then found a small cafe called the Devil's Sink Hole Grill. It appeared to be closed, but then he saw a sign in the window: "Go Around Back." Sam shrugged. He didn't have anything to lose—except maybe six thousand dollars and his life.

At the rear of the cafe he saw a couple of dented garbage cans stacked next to a flimsy red door. It was just as deserted here as it was on the street. Maybe the sign was for the garbage man.

Sam stood there for a moment in the dark silence, trying to decide whether to try the door. He could just see himself getting arrested again, picked up inside an empty restaurant on the beach in the middle of the night with six thousand dollars on him. He finally gave the door a push, more out of curiosity than anything else. The door opened and a sudden blast of noise hit Sam like an avalanche. Almost two hundred people were talking and laughing and dancing and eating. Eating? Hey, this was more like it!

A girl with curly hair and laughing eyes walked toward him. "Hominy in your potty?"

"Uh, just me."

She led him through the churning crowd to a tiny table next to the dance floor. A light from above shone down on it and Sam grimaced. "Excuse me, miss!" he shouted over the din. "Is this the only table you've got? It's awfully bright!"

"Sonly table!"

Sam's face sagged.

She gave him a smile, shifting a wad of chewing gum to her cheek. "Hey, whatcha care, good lookin guy like you? Yawta *be* on stage."

Sam was having trouble understanding her. Hunger and mental exhaustion were catching up to him. Also, his head was pounding and it was so noisy he could hardly hear her.

"'Sides, you don't wanna miss the show."

"Show?"

"Sure," she said. "Sheeza singer! Name's Donna Shorn!"

"Dinah Shore?"

She looked up at the ceiling, then back at Sam. "Rita Thorn!"

"Lena Horne?"

She said the words carefully this time, her mouth forming each syllable. "Tee-nuh For-LORNE!"

"Gotcha. Thanks."

She started away, then turned. "Brandy zoo you witch a gumball?"

"Huh?"

She shook her head and walked away.

Sam searched for a menu, but there was nothing on the table except a red-and-white checkered tablecloth, bathed in light.

"Take your order?" a waitress shouted in his ear.

"I don't know," Sam replied without looking up. "I didn't get a menu."

"All we have are steaks," she said, then her eyes went wide behind huge glasses with red lenses. "OhmyGod! Sam? Sam Durango?"

"Valerie?" he grinned. "Boy, you really get around."

"Me? What about you?"

"I just saw you last week at the Fish House."

"That was yesterday!"

"Oh."

"I like it better here. I'm making twice as much money. Remember? I even told you about this place."

Sam frowned. "Yeah. I mean, I sort of remember." His face brightened. "I'll make a deal with you. You bring me a nice big steak and I'll never forget anything you tell me again."

"Deal," she smiled. "You want a baked potato with that steak?"

"Fine."

Sam covered his eyes, warding off the light's glare, and watched Valerie until she disappeared into the crowd. His gaze shifted to the couples on the dance floor. He turned his head back to the table and THUNK. Sam's steak was in front of him.

"That was fast!"

"The cook owns the place. He likes to get 'em in, get 'em out."

Sam looked down at his plate. "Uh, would you do me one more favor?"

"Sure."

"Would you cut my steak up for me? It's kinda hard for me to do it with my arm in a sling."

"So that's why you didn't eat your lunch yesterday! What happened anyway?"

"Oh ... I wore it out from signing too many autographs."

She choked off a laugh. "I'll be right back." In an instant she returned and slid a plate in front of him. His steak was neatly diced into bite-sized cubes. Then she set down a fresh martini. "The table in the corner wants to buy you a drink."

"Thanks," Sam said, looking across the room. A man and

his wife were smiling at him. Sam lifted his glass and smiled back.

Suddenly the lights dimmed and the crowd grew silent. A man's voice crackled over the loudspeaker. "And now the Devil's Sink Hole Grill proudly presents miss Tina Forlorne!" Out from behind a curtain came a tall girl with long red hair and a slinky green dress, which accented the largest boobs Sam had ever seen. All the men in the room clapped and whistled. All the women sat quietly.

Valerie returned with another martini. She tried to whisper something in Sam's ear and pointed to a table in the middle of the room. Two men in cowboy clothes grinned at him. Sam smiled back.

Tina Forlorne stood alone in the middle of the dance floor, then started to sing in a soft whispery voice. "Blue skies, smiling at me, nothing but blue skies do I see. Blue days, all of them gone, nothing but blue skies from now on."

Music blasted suddenly and the curtain opened behind the dance floor. Revolving into view on a giant stage was an orchestra. The musicians were dressed in black, except for white gloves on their hands. The overhead lights went out and several black lights came on. All Sam saw were white gloves clapping and waving in the air.

"Never saw the sun shining so bright, never saw things going so right. Noticing the days hurrying by, when you're in love, my how they fly."

From out of the ceiling came a lighted carousel, carrying four men dressed in white. They joined Tina in song as the carousel slowly descended to the dance floor.

"Blue birds, singing a song, singing 'bout blue skies all day long."

The carousel lights winked off and blue spotlights came on. These were trained on a group of dancers who now whirled around the dance floor. The dancers and singers then knelt, forming a heart shape around Tina.

"Blue skies, smiling at me, nothing but blue skies do I see."

Giant movie screens blinked on. Here came images of mountains, waterfalls, forests, rivers, fountains, volcanoes, the Grand Canyon, Niagara Falls, outer space, the inside of an atom, the Great Barrier Reef, the statue of David, the Sistine Chapel, the Tower of Pisa, the Mona Lisa, the Taj Mahal, the Las Vegas skyline.

"Blue days, all of them gone, nothing but blue skies from now on."

Fireworks began to go off, and a sky rocket went sailing over Sam's head, bursting in a shower of red and yellow streamers that floated lazily onto the dance floor.

"Never saw the sun shining so bright, never saw things going so right. Noticing the days hurrying by, when you're in love, my how they fly."

Now a solitary spotlight shone on Tina Forlorne, and she finished the song alone.

"Blue birds, singing a song, singing 'bout blue skies all day long."

As her last note ended, the house lights came up, and the room exploded in applause. "Thank you! Thank you!" Tina cried, then she walked toward Sam's table. "And now I'd like to introduce a celebrity here with us tonight. Ladies and gentlemen, Mister Sam Du-RANG-o!"

All the women in the room began to clap and whistle. All the men sat quietly.

"Say a couple of words, Sam," Tina said, thrusting a microphone into his face.

"Howdy, folks."

Tina waved at the crowd and slipped behind the curtain. Everyone applauded, including Sam. Surprisingly, he felt no pain in his right shoulder now. In fact, he felt nothing at all.

Valerie appeared, carrying a martini in each hand. She motioned to a table off to the left and to a table off to the right. Sam nodded to the left, then to the right.

"You make a darn good martooni," he slurred, sipping from one and carefully setting the other on top of his steak.

"Owner makes 'em. It's his own recipe. Instead of gin he uses tequila, and instead of vermouth he uses vodka. You know?"

"I know. Well, I din know, but I know now. And how." She smiled.

Sam closed one eye so he could see her more clearly. "Time get off?"

"Hmm?"

"What—time—do you—get off?"

"Here, sign this," she said, holding out a pen and paper. "One of the couples who bought you a drink wants your autograph."

Sam squinted at the paper and signed his name carefully.

Sam looked up at Valerie. "Take you home?" he mumbled.

"Can't," she said softly. "My boyfriend's coming to get me. In fact, here he is now."

Sam tried to focus his eyes. Damn it, it was the highway patrolman who'd arrested him yesterday!

Or was it the day before yesterday?

"Ossifer," Sam said, getting to his feet and weaving toward the exit.

The girl with curly hair and laughing eyes saw him coming. "Sam a french a boodie?" she said.

"Where's—thuh—" Sam opened the back door and fell flat on his face.

7

Sam stood at the end of a bowling alley, nine other cow-boys grouped around him, all standing ramrod straight.

Two
Behind him
Three behind them
And four behind the other three.

He heard a low rumbling noise. A huge black cannonball rolled toward him. He tried to run, but couldn't move. He screamed.

"Sam. Sam! Wake up!"

His eyes popped open. Valerie's face swam into view. He closed his eyes. Valerie? It wasn't possible. He opened his eyes again, and this time saw Tina's face. He closed his eyes. What would Tina be doing in his motorhome? He opened his eyes a third time, and saw a girl with curly hair and laughing eyes.

"Yawl right?" she asked him.

Sam blinked, then realized with dismay that he'd lost his other contact lens. Squinting, he could make out his bed with a white sheet pulled up to his stomach. Well, that was a relief. At least the sheet wasn't pulled over his head.

It was no dream. There was Valerie, and Tina, and Curly. No, he couldn't call her Curly. When he thought of Curly, he thought of the bald Curly, which made him think of his station wagon, which make him think of Monica. Nope—it wasn't Curly.

"What's your name?" he asked her thickly.

"Curly."

"Uh, can I call you something else?"

"Well, my real name's Gilda."

"Hi, Gilda. Throw me my pants, Valerie. Is there any coffee, Tina?"

"Whyncha take a shower?" Gilda asked.

"And then get dressed," Valerie ordered.

"And then we'll talk," Tina added.

Sam wrapped the sheet around him and started to the bathroom. At the door he turned and gave them all a weak smile. Valerie's hair was down, falling in golden waves over her brown shoulders. Gilda wore a loose-fitting purple robe, and he got a glimpse of a creamy patch of thigh. Tina's hair was down, too, but there was something different about her today. Son of a gun! Her boobs were gone. All three were absolutely gorgeous, like ripe peaches hanging from a tree.

"See yuh," they said in unison.

After Sam showered, he slipped on his clothes and dropped his arm sling in the wastebasket. His shoulder still ached, but a cup of hot coffee and he would be as good as new. The three girls were at the table playing Monopoly. Sam poured himself some coffee and sat down.

Valerie looked him over. "You didn't put your thing back on."

"Yeah, I don't think I need it anymore. My arm feels a lot better today."

Tina smiled at him as she shook the dice. "I haven't met you officially. I'm Tina."

"Yes, I heard you sing at the club last night. You're very good."

"Thank you." She rolled the dice and they landed on double fives. "Doubles again?" Gilda cried. "One more time and you go to jail."

The mention of the word "jail" made Sam shiver and he reached shakily for his coffee cup. He gazed slowly around the neat little kitchen. He was still having trouble focusing with both contact lenses gone, but for some reason a wave of nostalgia washed over him. Something was familiar about this place, something bubbling up from a swampy corner of his brain, but he couldn't quite place it.

The girls shouted. Tina had rolled doubles a third time and decided she didn't want to play anymore. She flipped the board over, peppering Sam with little green houses and red hotels. Gilda and Valerie yelled at her in unison.

"Simmer down, simmer down," Sam pleaded. "I've got an overhang. I mean, a hangover."

"Yeah, and no wonder," Valerie said. "Do you know how many drinks you had last night?"

"A few."

"I counted them. You had eight double martinis. That's the same as fourteen regular martinis."

"I was celebrating," Sam said. He was celebrating Independence Day, for starters. After all, he was about as independent as he could get. He was celebrating the end of Labor Day, thanks to Jay Cohen. He wouldn't have any more presents to buy on Christmas Day or Valentine's Day, courtesy of one Monica Gibson Durango, which in a way made it Thanksgiving Day. And on Halloween Day Monica could hop on her broom and head for the Milky Way.

"What time is it?" Tina asked.

Sam turned his wrist to look at his watch and coffee splashed on the table. The girls ran for paper towels, Sam trying to watch all three at the same time. Maybe it was just as well he spilled his coffee. There was a little green house in the bottom of his cup.

The girls cleaned the table and put away the game. Sam went to the coffee pot and filled his cup again. Trying to focus with both eyes half shut, the strength suddenly went out of his legs.

"Tina! Valerie! Gilda! I've got something to show you, and you ain't gonna believe it. Not in a million years."

"What is it?" Valerie cried, rushing to his side.

"I used to live here," he announced, gesturing around the bungalow.

"Where?"

"Here. Right here in this house."

All three girls laughed.

"I'm serious. It was about ten years ago, when I was doing 'Cactus Classics.' And I was living right here in this house."

Tina grinned. "I used to watch that show at my grandma's."

The other two were giving him skeptical looks.

"All right, I'll prove it to you," Sam said. "Buck Beaumont was living with me at the time, and one night I carved my initials on the back of the closet door. Come on, I'll show you."

They followed him down the hall to the bedroom. He flung open the closet. "Now it's gotta be here somewhere, unless the door's been changed. Ah HA!" Sam found the initials, right where he remembered, but they did not read S. D. anymore. The S had been blatantly changed to a B and the D was changed to another B. Instead of S. D. the initials read B. B. That sonuvabitchin' Buck Beaumont had done it again.

The girls walked back to the kitchen, Sam quietly following behind. They didn't seem impressed with his discovery, but for Sam it was like going back in time. He was a promising young actor again instead of a washed-up television star. He was twenty-nine instead of thirty-nine, and every day was a brand new adventure. But just how did a guy explain all that to three juicy young peaches?

Tina said something about a rehearsal at the club and left the room to get dressed. Meanwhile, Gilda and Valerie were setting up a Scrabble game at the table. "I want to thank you for taking care of me last night," he said to them. "I usually don't drink that much."

Tina came back into the room. She looked different again.

Son of a gun, her boobs were back. "Are you coming to the club tonight, Sam? I'm doing a new song."

"Not tonight," Sam laughed. "I need a day off."

"It's my day off, too," Gilda said. "Maybe we kin do somethin later. Swear you goin?"

Sam was at the door. "Oh, I don't know. I thought I'd take a walk down the beach and get my feet wet. If you come down later, look for me. I'll be the only one without a suntan."

"Sam?" It was Valerie. "Did you lose something last night?"

He looked at her blankly. She opened her hand, revealing a wrinkled cashier's check and a wad of bills. "This fell out of your pants when we were putting you to bed last night."

"Thanks," Sam said. "Gimme a twenty and hold onto the rest of it for me, will yuh? And don't lose it!"

He rolled his pants legs up to the knees and started down the beach. Maybe the fresh air would ease the knot in his stomach. He didn't know whether it was all the drinking he did the night before or being around three beautiful girls and smelling their smells in the beach house, but Sam was beginning to feel like an old man.

When he was younger, things were different. He would look at older people as though they were aliens from another planet. Actually, he didn't look at them; he looked through them. It never dawned on him that they had the same feelings and emotions as he did. Now here he was, getting marked off by the calendar, half his life gone already, and there wasn't a damn thing he could do about it.

A small girl in an orange sun dress walked toward him. She appeared to be about seven years old. In her hand was a small purse. "Excuse me, mister. Can I have a nickel?"

Sam grinned, searching in his pocket and coming up with a fifty-cent piece. "Do you have any change?"

The girl opened her purse, the sun glinting off a silvery mound of coins inside. She took Sam's fifty cents and counted out nine nickels in change, giving them to him one at a time.

"Thanks, mister."

Now she spoke to another man. "Excuse me, mister. Can I have a nickel?"

Sam ventured near the water, where the sand was damp and cool. White suds lathered his feet as the surf splashed around him and sea gulls screeched overhead. On the horizon he saw the tiny outline of a tanker. He inhaled deeply, feeling the tension ooze out of his body. How he loved the ocean, and the way it made him feel—as long as he watched it heave and roll while sand was packed firmly beneath his feet.

Back before "Cactus Classics," he had a bit part in a war movie that was filmed on an aircraft carrier. Sam got so seasick that a helicopter was dispatched to take him to a hospital on the mainland. Then he got so airsick that the helicopter was forced to land, and he was transferred to an ambulance. If they hadn't stuck an I-V in his arm, he might have died from dehydration.

Sam groped in his pockets for his cigarette fixings. Damn! The cops had taken them. Well, maybe he could buy some more. There used to be a little bar around here somewhere, but it was probably gone now. When "Cactus Classics" was popular, he went there all the time and he'd take a different girl to the bungalow every night. All those girls, Sam smiled wistfully. By now they were married with families, and they probably never gave him a second thought.

On the other side of the road Sam saw a small grocery store. A bell tinkled as he went inside. Half a dozen people were lined up in front of the cash register, where a man behind the counter rang up purchases.

"Your total comes to twelve seventy-five. Next. Nine thirty-eight. Next. Four ninety-two. Next. Fifty-eight cents. Next."

It was Sam's turn. "Yeah, give me a pouch of smoking tobacco, please, and a pack of cigarette papers."

"Here you go. That'll be fifteen forty-nine."

"Fifteen forty-nine?"

"Two forty-nine for the tobacco, thirteen dollars for the Zig Zags. Next."

Sam paid for everything with his twenty dollar bill, then started down the beach again. He found a quiet spot near the water and began to roll himself a smoke.

"Saaaaaamm!"

Someone was calling him from off in the distance. He saw a dot far down the beach, and gradually the dot materialized into the figure of a young woman. It was Gilda! Sam ran to meet her. She waved at him, and he waved back, running faster.

He passed an elderly couple walking hand in hand. He looked at them, but he never really saw them. In fact, he looked right through them. He bumped into the small girl wearing an orange sun dress. Her tiny purse flew open and hundreds of flat shiny objects scattered into the sand.

"Gilda!" he cried, his heart beating strongly in his chest. He felt as though he were a young Indian brave, loping across the prairie in his bare feet, following the buffalo.

Youth. Fleeting elusive youth. It was all in one's mind. A man was as young as he felt. As young as he ... as young as ... young ...

Sam couldn't catch his breath. His heart pounded and his legs itched, and he was getting a headache. His run slowed to a trot, and the trot to a walk. By the time Gilda reached his side, he stood bent over with his hands on his knees.

"You okay?" she asked, not even breathing hard.

"Minute," Sam gasped. "Gimme ... minute."

Sam and Gilda returned to the beach house. He took another shower, then walked into the kitchen. She was at the counter stirring a bowl of eggs, and a skillet of bacon sizzled on the stove.

"You didn't have to do that," he said. "We could have gone out."

"I don't mind," she smiled, not looking up. "Shoot, I love to cook."

"I'll set the table," he said, going to the cupboard and taking out three plates.

"Yonly need two," she said. "Valerie's gone. Hasta work."

Sam put the dishes on the table and sat down. A sheet of paper lay there, and Sam gave it a curious look. It was the score sheet from Valerie and Gilda's Scrabble game. Valerie had won, twenty-eight to nineteen.

Gilda brought the food to the table and dished it into the plates. Before she could sit down, Sam jumped to his feet and pulled out her chair.

"Thanks, Sam," Gilda smiled. "No one zever done that for me before."

He gave her a grin and stuck a strip of bacon in his mouth. "No one's ever fixed me breakfast for dinner before."

"Who'd ever believe it?" she murmured, shaking her head. "Me, eatin bacon and eggs with Sam Durango."

"Well, I can't think of anyone I'd rather be dining with, Gilda. You're a very attractive young woman and a damn good cook."

"Kin I ask you somethin?"

"Sure."

"You married?"

"Kind of."

"What's that mean?"

"It means I—didn't get my option picked up."

"So what are you gonna do?"

"Well, the first thing I'm going to do is enjoy this pleasant little repast with you."

"Okay, but you'd better eat first."

Sam sipped his coffee, eyeing Gilda over the top of his cup. "Now it's my turn to ask a question."

"Whatcha wanna know?"

"For one thing, I'm curious as to why you don't like your name. I think Gilda's a pretty name."

Gilda turned up her nose. "Sawful. Sounds so old-fashioned."

"I don't think so, and I'm not old-fashioned," Sam answered, gingerly dabbing at his mouth with a napkin.

"Well, I do. And you know what?"

"What?"

"I gotta sister. Her name's Hilda, and she hates her name, too. She's livin with a guy in San Diego."

"But surely you don't plan on calling yourself Curly for the rest of your life?"

"I dunno," she shrugged. "Never thought about it."

"Well, I like the name Gilda," Sam repeated. "It reminds me of a movie I saw when I was a kid."

"Oh yeah?"

"It was a real classic. Rita Hayworth was in it."

"Who?"

"Never mind. Here, I'll help you do the dishes."

It was late. Sam was stretched out on the couch, his hands behind his head, while Gilda finished in the kitchen. Lying there, full of food and at peace with the world, life made a lot more sense to him. Clint Eastwood had his restaurant, Roy Rogers had his museum, Gene Autry had his star in the sidewalk. But Sam had them all beat. For the moment, anyway, he had his own little place, right here on the couch, in a bungalow on the beach, and no one could ever hurt him again.

Gilda came into the room. Sam watched her in the dim light, a hard lump in his throat. She looked ravishing in her clinging Levis and halter top.

"What do you feel like doing?" he asked her.

"I dunno."

"Want to go to a movie?"

"Naw."

"Want to go for a walk?"

"Naw."

"Want to go to the club?"

"Gawd, no."

"Well, tell me then."

"Well ... why don't I take a nice hot bath ..."

"Uh huh," Sam whispered huskily.

"Slip into somethin comfortable ..."

"Hunh," Sam whispered.

"And then mebbe we kin play a game ... or somethin."

"Hnnnnnnhh," Sam whispered.

Soon he heard water running in the tub and sniffed the faint aroma of White Shoulders perfume. He loved that scent. It reminded him of the first girl he ever really liked. Her name was Rosalee. He couldn't even remember her last name. Once, on her birthday, Sam gave her a small bottle of White Shoulders. She was thrilled. Thanked him over and over again. So he asked her to go to the movies with him, but she had a date. He asked her out again. She had a date. Funny. He never did go out with her. Wonder whatever happened. To Rosalee.

Gilda slipped into the room, moonlight gently glimmering through her sheer negligee. "Sam?" she asked softly.

Sam was sound asleep on the couch.

Sam yawned. He was on the couch and bright sunshine streamed through the open window. He stretched, his spine cracking in six places. Voices were coming from the kitchen. He climbed into his pants and struggled into his shirt. "Good morning," he said to the girls, and headed for the coffee pot.

"Hi, cowboy," Valerie said.

"Hi, cowboy," Tina said.

"Hello, Sam," Gilda said coolly.

The girls were seated at the table playing a game of backgammon. Sam got his coffee and walked over. "Who's winning?"

"Valerie is," Gilda said. "Thonly way that Tina kin win is she hasta roll double sixes this time."

Tina shook the dice and let them fly. "Come on, boxcars!" she cried. The dice thumped down the board and landed on two sixes.

"You ought to go to Vegas, girl," Sam said.

"I know," Tina laughed. "I've always been lucky at dice."

As the girls set up the board for another game, Sam walked to the window and looked out at the ocean. "What's everybody doing today?"

Gilda was shaking the dice. "I gotta work."

"So do I," Tina said.

"I don't," Valerie said. "What did you want to do?"

"Oh, I don't know. I thought I'd hit the beach again. There

used to be a little place down there where I spent a lot of time. I thought I'd see if I could find it again."

"What kind of place?"

"A little bar, right on the beach. It wasn't that far from here."

"Hmm, the only one I can think of around here is Billy Bob's Booze Barn. They've got sandwiches and all kinds of neat drinks. Everybody goes there."

"Sounds good to me."

Valerie vanished into the bedroom. When she returned, she was wearing a white one-piece bathing suit, white sandals, and a white beach robe. Sam stared at her with his mouth open.

"Yawl have fun," Gilda said and winked at Valerie.

"Bye," Tina smiled. "Come on, ten the hard way!" The dice rolled down the board, landing on two fives.

Sam and Valerie started out the door, Sam squinting into the sun. "Boy, that sun's bright today. Wish I had some sunglasses."

"I've got an extra pair," Valerie said, tugging them out of her pocket and passing them to him. The glasses were fitted with tiny rose-colored lenses, and when Sam put them on he felt like he was at a 3-D movie. Still, they were better than nothing.

They walked across the sand, cutting diagonally toward the water. It was a weekend, and the beach was crowded. Children were building sand castles and yelling at each other in high-pitched authoritative voices. Boys in black wetsuits skimmed across the waves on surfboards, girls in bikinis walked slowly along the water's edge, and seagulls screeched overhead, looking for handouts.

Sam felt out of place, with his pants rolled up to the knees and rose-colored glasses barely covering his eyes. When he looked next to him, however, and saw Valerie so close he could smell her toothpaste, nothing else mattered.

She touched his arm. "We've got company."

A man in his mid-thirties was coming toward them, his hand already outstretched. His hair was in a crewcut and he wore a baggy red swimsuit. There was a woman with him whose hair was in curlers, each a different color. She was pretty, but she looked tired for some reason.

The man and woman were surrounded by five small children.

"I don't believe it," the man smiled proudly. "Sam Durango! My name's Buddy, and this here's my wife Marcie."

"Howdy, folks," Sam said, peering at them over the top of Valerie's sunglasses.

Buddy was still shaking Sam's hand. "And this is Dee Dee, and John John, and Lulu, and Fifi, and Horatio. Named after his grandfather," Buddy explained.

"Where's Mimi?" Marcie asked, looking around.

"We're from Kansas," Buddy went on. "Out here on vacation. And you're the first movie star we've seen."

"TV star."

"TV star. Could we—do you think we could get your autograph, Mister Durango? Love to show it to the folks back home."

"I don't have anything to write with."

Buddy made a face. "Me, either. Well, how about a picture then? Maybe I could get your daughter to take one of us together, you and me and Marcie and the kids."

"Sure," Sam said, winking at Valerie. He bent and gave her a long passionate kiss. Her eyes went wide before they closed. She wrapped her arms tightly around him, pressing her body close.

Buddy laughed with glee. "Hollywood! I love it!"

Valerie, a little breathless, took the camera from Buddy and looked into the viewfinder. "All right, everybody. Get a little closer together. A little closer. Okay, hold it."

Click.

"Got it," Valerie said. She and Sam waved goodbye and started down the beach again.

"That was some kiss, Sam," she said, folding her hand into his.

"Yeah. Look, I know you've got a boyfriend and all. But

when that guy called you my daughter—well, I just couldn't help myself. You're not mad, are you?"

"Mad? Of course not. Besides, Clyde isn't really my boyfriend."

"Clyde?"

"Yes. You met him at the club the other night, remember?"

"I think so. I'm not sure."

"He's a highway patrolman, works all over the county. I just call him my boyfriend to keep the wolves away."

"Ahh-OOOOH!" Sam howled.

Valerie laughed, then squeezed his hand. "Look, there it is!" She pointed at a rustic wooden building down the beach. Over the door, on a piece of faded driftwood, hung the peeling picture of a mermaid. Sam barely made out the words "billy BOB's Booze barN."

Valerie stared up at him, a questioning look on her face. "Well, is this the place you remember or not?"

He shrugged. Ten years was a mighty long time, and he just couldn't place it.

They entered through a rickety screen door. Against the side of the big room was a long bar. Two wooden fans cranked slowly, and a faint breeze stirred up dust motes. The room was empty except for the bartender, who was studying a racing form on the counter.

Sam winked at Valerie again. "DRINKS FOR EVERYBODY ON ME!" he hollered.

Instantly forty-five heads popped up. A smaller bar several steps down from the main one overlooked the ocean, and it was crowded with people.

"Gin and tonic," one head called out. "Whiskey sour," ordered another. "Cuba Libre." "Tom Collins." "Moscow mule." "Planter's punch." "Gin fizz." "Brandy Alexander." "Singapore sling." "Mint julep." "Bloody Mary."

Sam hoped the bill wouldn't exceed six thousand dollars. "Give me some money," he whispered to Valerie. All he had in his pocket were nine nickels.

She laughed as she took out her wallet. "What are you going to have, big spender?"

"I think I'll take it easy today," he answered, turning to the bartender. "Double martini on the rocks, hold the olive."

The bartender turned to Valerie. "I'll have a virgin, please." He set a tall glass of champagne in front of her. There was a cherry in it.

Valerie wrinkled her nose and tapped her glass against his. "To a beautiful day," she smiled. When she set the glass down there was foam on her nose, and Sam fought the urge to kiss it away.

The bartender left. It was just Valerie and Sam, alone at the bar. "So what's it like being a famous movie star?" she asked him quietly.

"TV star."

"You were in some movies, too. I saw you."

"Boy, you must be some fan. I wasn't even in the credits."

"I've always been your fan."

Sam studied his drink. "I'm not a star. Not anymore. My show got canceled, and the studio paid me off. I'm just another Joe, looking for a job."

"I'm sorry, Sam. I didn't know."

"You don't have to be sorry. I knew it would happen someday. I just didn't expect it to happen quite so soon."

"You'll get another show. I bet your agent is working on it right now."

"I don't think so," Sam sighed. "In fact, he dropped me, too."

"Why?" she asked, a look of concern on her face.

"Well, I'm not sure exactly. We had an argument. I said something I shouldn't have. He got mad. And that was that."

"Oh, maybe not. Maybe he's not mad anymore. Maybe he's already tried to call you back, and he can't find you. I mean, does anyone know where you are, Sam?"

"Well, now that you mention it, no, no one does. Except you."

She smiled softly. "It'll work out, you'll see." There was a pause, then she said, "Do you want to know something?"

"Sure."

"You're going to think this is silly, but sometimes I get goosebumps when I'm around you."

"Why?" he swallowed.

"Because people are always coming up to you and asking you for your autograph and stuff. Like today on the beach. And it makes me feel kind of famous, too. I like that feeling. I always have."

"Excuse me."

It was the bartender. "Could I get you to sign this for me, Mister Durango?" He thrust a menu in front of Sam, then added hastily, "It's not for me, it's for my wife."

"What's her name?"

"Uh ... Irving."

Sam scratched his name on the top of the men, then pushed it back across the bar.

"Thanks a lot," the bartender said, backing away.

Valerie was shaking her head. "See? It never stops."

Sam laughed and popped an ice cube in his mouth. He was in a romantic mood, and the drink had nothing to do with it. It was Valerie. He couldn't keep his eyes off of her. Her hair, and her lips, and her slender fingers, and the fragile swell of her breasts against the tight restraints of her robe, which would give way to the slightest whisper of a breeze—

"Sam? What are you thinking about?"

"You," he sighed. "You're beautiful. With a figure like yours, you shouldn't be wearing that skimpy bathing suit. It's enough to make a grown man cry."

"I wore it for you."

The bar was filling up and getting noisy. "Bartender!" he called. "Give me a bottle of gin and a bottle of champagne. And a little thing of them cherries. We gotta go."

The bartender frowned. "We can only sell them by the drink, Mister Durango. State law. I could get in a lot of trouble."

Sam held his hand out to Valerie. She opened her wallet and dropped one of his fifty dollar bills on the counter. Sam's eyes bulged, but it was too late.

The bartender wet his lips and began filling a paper sack. "I think I'll go see if anybody needs another drink," he said, giving Sam an exaggerated wink.

By the time he and Valerie got outside it was beginning to get dark. "Let's find a little cove or something," he whispered. "I want to be alone with you."

"I know a place," she said. "It's my secret place. Nobody else knows about it."

She was a step in front of him, leading him along the water's edge. They came to a cluster of small boulders and climbed over them. On the other side was a clearing in the sand that stretched to the water. Valerie shrugged out of her robe and spread it on the soft sand.

Sam brought out the bottles. "One for you," he said, handing her the champagne. "One for me." He screwed the cap off the gin. "One for you." He placed a cherry in her mouth. "One for me." His mouth was on hers.

He heard a rushing in his ears, but it wasn't the surf. It was his blood boiling. His hands fumbled at the clasp on her bathing suit, and then he moved the zipper down as far as it would go.

"Hold me," she whispered.

He put his arms around her, then kissed her gently. Sam

was not religious, but if there was a God and a heaven, they were both right here. Valerie groaned softly and her arms tightened around his neck.

"I love you," he thought he heard her say. But maybe it was just the wind.

Sam opened his eyes. He was back on the couch, the sheet over him and the room flooded with sunlight. He sat up and rubbed his face. On the table was a half-empty bottle of gin.

His head throbbed and there were scratches across his chest. Then he remembered Valerie and last night on the beach, and a warm glow came over him. He stepped into his pants and slowly buttoned his shirt. Entering the kitchen, he made a beeline for the coffee pot. The girls were at the table playing dominoes.

"Hi, cowboy," Tina smiled.

"Hello, Sam," Gilda said.

"Good morning, handsome," Valerie cooed.

"Morn," Sam mumbled. "Anybody got a cigarette?"

Tina handed him one that she was smoking. It was hand-rolled and had a pungent aroma. "Hey, you roll your own, too." He inhaled and immediately began to cough. "What the hell you smoking, girl? Coffee grounds?"

"Take it easy," Tina grinned. "All you need is one hit."

Sam groped for a chair and sat down heavily. His head spun like a top and his ears rang. "So what's everybody doing today?"

Tina said, "Rehearsal."

"Oh." He saw the back of another girl at the kitchen sink. "What about you?"

"Rehearsal," she said, turning around. It was Tina!

He turned to the girl next to him. "How did she—?" Son of a gun, it was Tina! Sam began to slowly slide off the chair, a blank smile on his face.

"Sam! Sam!" Tina cried, shaking him. "Snap out of it. There's someone at the door. You've got to be cool."

"Cool? Hell, I'm ice cold."

He closed his eyes and saw colorful paisley patterns swirling around and around. That was sure some funny tobacco! He opened his eyes again and was looking into the eyes of the biggest highway patrolman he'd ever seen. Sam held up his arms. "I didn't do it!" he cried. "She did it, and she tried to make me do it, but I didn't do it."

"Sam, relax," somebody said. He tried to focus. It was Tina. "This is Clyde. Remember? You met him at the club the other night."

"Hi, Sam," Clyde grinned, shoving an outstretched hand toward him.

"Officer," Sam said, gripping the man's hand for dear life.

"Cut out that 'officer' bullshit. Call me Clyde."

"Want some coffee?" Tina asked him.

"Naw, I can't stay. Some idiot parked a motorhome down by your club three days ago, and the damn thing's still sittin' there, takin' up two parking spaces. I'm gonna have to git a tow truck and haul it out of there. It's got every merchant on the block pissed off."

Sam was getting that familiar knot in his stomach again. "Officer," he said weakly.

"Clyde," Clyde cried.

"Clyde," Sam sighed. "Let me ask you something. Is that motorhome white with a red stripe down the side?"

"Yeah, I think so."

"And is there an orange stripe over the red stripe?"

"Yeah."

Sam tried to smile. "That's my motorhome. I forgot all about it."

The girls scurried around Sam, helping him out of the chair, on with his boots, down with his pants legs. Clyde paced the room, barking orders. "Git his hair combed! Pour some coffee down him! Tuck his shirt tail in!"

They got him to the front door, leaning him against it like a Christmas tree. "It's no use," Clyde grumbled. "One of you better go with us."

"I've gotta work," Gilda said.

"So do I," Valerie frowned.

"I'll go," Tina said. "Just give me a minute to change."

Clyde drove Tina and Sam in his cruiser, the police radio turned up all the way. With a screech of brakes, he pulled to a stop next to Sam's motorhome. A thick wad of pink parking tickets was wedged under the windshield wiper. Clyde had his hand out.

"Fifty bucks and I'll take care of it."

Sam wearily went into his pocket. Damn, Valerie still had all his money. "Uh, can I pay you later? I left my money at home."

Tina opened her purse. "Here, I've got it." Sam smiled gratefully. "It's okay, Sam. I owe Gilda fifty, so you can pay her."

"Great. I'll get it from Valerie."

Clyde shook his head, then stuck the money in his pocket. Sam and Tina climbed out of the car, but Clyde continued to scrutinize Sam through baleful eyes. "Don't I know you from somewheres?"

Tina shifted uncomfortably. There was a long line of cars behind Clyde's cruiser, and horns were starting to blow.

"I used to be on TV," Sam offered.

"That ain't it," Clyde said, the noise muffling his words. "Seems like I seen you somewheres else."

Tina yelled to make herself heard. "HE WAS AT THE CLUB THE OTHER NIGHT!"

"I KNOW, BUT I SEEN HIM SOMEWHERES ELSE."

Sam shrugged, taking Tina's arm and leading her to the motorhome. Clyde slowly adjusted his sunglasses and tipped the visor of his cap forward. The cruiser squealed away, leaving rubber down the pavement for almost a block.

Sam laughed as he unlocked the motorhome. "It's a wonder he didn't have his damn siren on." Then he heard a police siren as Clyde's cruiser turned the corner.

He got behind the wheel and drove down the street. Tina rolled her window down and let the wind blow in her face. "This is nice," she sighed. "Someday, when I get my own band, I'm going to buy a motorhome. I'll be able to travel all over the country and never have to stay in a hotel room."

"Sounds good," Sam said. "Where to, anyway? I mean, for right now."

Tina looked at her watch. "I've got a rehearsal with the band, and after that I'm free for the rest of the afternoon."

"Great."

"Turn right at the intersection. Okay, take another right. Now take another right. Stop."

Sam was back at the club. He put nine nickels in the parking meter and followed Tina inside. The orchestra was setting up their instruments on the revolving stage. Singers rehearsed in the corner, while a group of dancers practiced their steps. A lighting technician adjusted a spotlight, the audio engineer checked the sound level, and another man took rockets out of a box marked "Danger! High Explosives."

Tina strolled to the dance floor. The lights overhead accentuated her flaming red hair. She was dressed in a pair of skintight green pants and a tight green sweater, with a green jade necklace dangling from her neck. And son of a gun, Sam grinned as he settled into a chair, she was wearing her boobs today.

"All right, let's try it, guys," Tina said, striding to the microphone, her voice echoing through the room. "Everybody to their places, and we'll take it on three. One—two—three."

The lights went completely out, and then a green spotlight hit the middle of the far wall, illuminating a fire extinguisher. The light veered off to the right, moved across Tina, and came to rest on the sign leading to the men's room.

It didn't faze Tina, who went right into her song. "When whippoorwills call, and evening is nigh, I hurry to my—" SQUAWWWK!

Feedback from a nearby speaker made Sam clamp his hands over his ears. The engineer turned a knob and the screeching subsided.

"All right," Tina said. "Let's try it again. One—two—three." The green spotlight shifted from the men's room sign to Tina's knees.

"When whippoorwills call, and evening is nigh, I hurry to my blue heaven. A turn to the right, a little white light will lead you to my blue heaven."

Here came the revolving stage as the orchestra broke into music. The stage didn't stop, however, but kept rotating until the orchestra was out of sight again. Sam heard muffled music from deep within the bowels of the building.

A lighted carousel wobbled from the ceiling, stopping two feet from the dance floor. Then one of the cables holding it came undone, and the carousel careened sideways, spilling four singers to the floor.

Meanwhile, the dancers rushed out, but in the semi-darkness they didn't see the singers sprawled around Tina. There was a crashing noise as dancers fell upon singers, but Tina continued to sing.

"You'll see a smiling face, a fireplace, a cozy room. A little nest that's nestled where the roses bloom."

Giant movie screens blinked on. Sam was waiting for the Grand Canyon, Niagara Falls, the Mona Lisa, Las Vegas. Instead he got a black-and-white slide show from somebody's old photo album: a man standing in front of a pickup truck, a young boy eating watermelon, a dog wearing a birthday hat, an upside-down photograph of a baby in a high chair.

The screens suddenly went dark and a skyrocket flashed past Sam, missing him by inches. It smashed into the far wall, sending sparks flying across the room. Tina crouched down and finished the song, just as the spotlight focused on her face.

"Just Tommy and me, and baby makes three. We're happy in my blue heaven."

The lights came on, and Sam clapped hollowly.

"Okay, that's a wrap!" Tina called. "Good work, everybody. See you tonight."

They reached the motorhome just as it began to sprinkle. Sam drove quietly while Tina directed him to a rustic cafe. For some reason, Sam was famished. She didn't say anything about the rehearsal, and neither did Sam. Besides, with a body like hers she didn't need dancers and rockets.

By the time they finished eating, the sky was filled with dark clouds and rain was slashing down in silvery sheets. Tina grabbed his hand, and they raced back to the motorhome, whooping and hollering as the rain soaked them to the skin. Sam helped her inside, then slammed the door shut behind them with a bang. Tina stood next to him, hugging herself in the dim light. "I've got to get out of these things," she said. "I can't afford to catch a cold."

"Yeah, I'm a little mildewy myself," he answered, pulling off his wet shirt.

"What's that?" she asked, looking at the scratches on Sam's chest.

"That? Oh, I always get those when I drink martinis. Some kind of— uh— reaction to pimentos or something. I dunno."

"Oh," she said. "Well, I'll be right back." She started toward the small bathroom at the back of the motorhome. "Why don't you close the curtains while I'm gone? And maybe put on some nice music."

"Okay." Sam smiled. Whoa! He'd never tripped the light fantastic in a parking lot before. He turned on the radio, then went to work closing up the motorhome. Afterwards, he sat down on the couch and began removing his spongy cowboy boots. Just then he heard a throaty rumble from outside and peered through the window. Pulling into the parking lot was a Bluebird Wanderlodge, one of the most beautiful motorhomes Sam had ever seen.

"Wow," he sighed. "Look at that."

Tina, clad only in a shimmering pair of green panties and a monstrous green brassiere, had opened the bathroom door and was walking toward him in the dim light. "Oh, Sam, it's just me."

"Check out those headlights," Sam whispered as he stared at the big motorhome.

"Oh, Sam."

"And just look at that beautiful rear end. The only thing missing is a trailer hitch."

Tina blushed. Her arms slowly went behind her back, then she dropped the brassiere. Sam heard it crash as it hit the floor.

When he saw her, he suddenly forgot all about the motorhome outside. What a striking woman she was. Long silky legs. Softly rounded hips. Blonde fuzz on her stomach, running down in a faint line. As the music played softly on the radio, Sam gently took her in his arms.

"You've been listening to the music of Mantovani," the radio announcer said. "And now it's time for the seven o'clock news. Two convicts …"

"Did he say seven o'clock?" Tina asked, pushing Sam away.

"Yeah."

"Oh no!" Tina cried. "I'm late for work! We've gotta go!"

Sam woke up in the motorhome. Sitting up slowly, he tried to sort everything in the jumble that filled his mind. The parking lot. Tina. Losing track of time. Getting to the club an hour late. Arriving back at the beach house and finding it completely deserted. Heading back to the motorhome. Sleeping in his own bed for the first time.

Now he got to his feet and walked to the bathroom, his mouth set in a tight frown. Valerie and Tina and Gilda were wonderful girls, lovely and willing and everything, and the last three days were like some kind of crazy dream. But dreams had a way of turning into nightmares if a person let them. If he were younger, or if the girls were older ... no, even then it wouldn't work out. Besides, the girls probably liked him for one reason: who he was, or rather, who he used to be.

Sam felt a tear on his cheek. One lousy lonely tear. He wished he really could cry, and that the tears would take away the pain of losing his wife, his job, his home, and everything he'd worked for all these years. Perhaps then it would be easier, because he knew that today was the day he had to make an important decision.

Unfortunately, every time Sam made a decision, nothing seemed to change. When someone else made a decision, the whole world wobbled off course. Look what happened just in the last week. Jay Cohen made a decision, and Sam was out of a job. Monica made a decision, and Sam was out of a marriage.

Larry Noble made a decision, and without an agent Sam was out of touch with the entire film industry.

Surely, he'd made some important decisions. Sam scratched the three-day growth on his chin as he thought about it. Well, he made the decision to sell the station wagon and buy the motorhome. That was a big one. But ... that was about it. Well, he was going to make another big decision. Right now.

He splashed his face with cold water, then ran a comb through his rapidly graying hair. The studio used a cheap water-based dye and every time he wet his hair more of the color washed out. That was okay with Sam. It would serve as a constant reminder of the make-believe world he'd left behind.

He opened his closet door and pulled out a wrinkled shirt and a wrinkled pair of pants. Both smelled faintly of chlorine. Then he climbed the steps of the beach house under a sky that was still heavy with rain clouds. He tried the door and it swung open. The girls were in the living room, watching an old movie on a portable television set.

"Hello, Sam," Tina said.

"Hello, Sam," Gilda said.

"Good morning, handsome," Valerie said.

"Hi. Any coffee?"

He walked back into the living room, cup in hand. Then he rubbed the stubble on his chin again. "Mind if I shave?"

Sam closed the bathroom door and opened a rusty medicine cabinet. He took out a razor, studied the blade for broken edges, then lathered his face with hand soap. First he shaved from his neck up to his chin, then from his bottom lip to his jaw. He brought the razor up over his top lip and stopped. How would he look with a moustache? Well, there was only one way to find out.

He searched through the cabinet for aftershave lotion, but all he could find was a small bottle of cologne. He patted some on his face, chuckling as he thought about it. The Vegas Kid was wearing perfume.

Sam opened the bathroom door, and the girls looked over at him.

"Did you sleep well in your little motor house?" Valerie asked him.

"Like a cowboy at roundup time," Sam grinned weakly.

Gilda was staring at him. "Are you growin a muh-stash?" Sam ran a finger over his top lip. "Yup, what do you think?" "I like a moustache on a guy," Tina said. "Makes you look kind of sill-voo-play."

Sam shifted his weight from one foot to the other and jabbed his thumbs in his pants pockets. He'd rehearsed a dramatic little speech while he shaved, but the words must have gone down the sink with his whiskers. He couldn't remember any of it now, especially with six beautiful eyes staring right at him.

"Uh, I gotta go. Goodbye."

Somehow, though, they must have understood what he was trying to say. The only one who showed any emotion was Valerie, who sat back slowly, a look of tender concern on her face.

"Well, shoot, Sam," Gilda said. "We didn't speck you to stay forever." Valerie, biting her lip, whispered, "You wouldn't be you if you were any other way." Tina deftly rolled a cigarette with one hand. "Here, take this with you."

"No, I better not," Sam said quickly. "Well ... adios. And thanks for everything."

All three girls ran to him. Gilda gave him a peck on the cheek, Valerie squeezed his hand, and Tina brought him sandwiches in a brown paper bag. Before he knew it, he was in the front seat of the motorhome and they were all waving. Then they were gone.

"Sam?" It was Valerie, back at the window.

"Did you forget something?"

He looked at her blankly. She held out her hand, and there was his wrinkled cashier's check and a wad of bills. "You told me to keep this for you, but I didn't think you meant forever."

"Oh," he said. What a sweetheart! "Thanks, Valerie." He

took the money, but held onto her hand. "I'm going to miss you, girl. I'm really going to miss—" He never got a chance to finish. She was on her tiptoes, kissing his lips, and in between kisses she was whispering, "Las Vegas, Sam—that's the—town for a—guy like you—mmm— Las Vegas. "

She backed away slowly, giving him one last brave smile. He turned on the engine and waved goodbye again, wishing desperately that he could shoot the scene all over again. For take two, the engine wouldn't start, the skies wouldn't be black, and he would walk back into the beach house, Valerie leading him by the hand. But this was real life, not a movie. The motorhome's engine idled in neutral, raindrops spattered on his windshield, and Valerie walked back into the beach house by herself.

He pulled away from the curb just as a black limousine glided to a stop next to the bungalow. Through his sideview mirror, he saw a short man dressed in dark clothing start up the sidewalk. Sam shook his head sadly as he drove down the road. It was probably one of Valerie's boyfriends, and here he thought … oh, to hell with what he thought. It didn't matter anymore.

He drove aimlessly along the beach road, not sure of his next move. He saw Billy Bob's Booze Barn over near the water, and he could make out the pile of boulders where Valerie had led him that night. Here was the stretch of beach where he ran to meet Gilda, and there was the little grocery store where he got his smoking tobacco.

He drove slowly past the Devil's Sink Hole Grill, almost tempted to stop in and wait until the girls arrived at work tonight. "It's me. I decided not to leave after all," he could say. Boy, would they be surprised. But that was stupid. He'd already told them goodbye, and now he had to go.

In a way, the whole thing was funny. He'd been so intent on making a long flowery speech, thinking they would sob and pull on him while he tried to get to the motorhome—and what happened? Hell, they'd practically thrown him out!

Sam saw a big shopping center and pulled in. He needed a

few things, like razor blades, aftershave lotion, and a pair of reading glasses. He also needed groceries and linens and paper towels and toilet paper, all the things that made a house a home. And he also had to make some phone calls.

He found a telephone booth and emptied his change on the counter. The first call was to his lawyer. No, Howe hadn't heard from Monica. Yes, he would keep Sam advised on the divorce proceedings, once Sam got some kind of mailing address. No, it was no trouble, no trouble at all.

Sam dropped another dime in the slot. Maybe what he ought to do was just talk to Monica himself. Maybe they were both being a little too hasty. Maybe they could talk this over like two adults. Maybe—

"Hello?" It was Monica. "Hello?" she said again. Sam's voice caught in his throat. He couldn't even breathe. "Is there someone there? Hello?" He quietly put the phone down.

Another dime dropped, and this time Larry Noble's secretary answered. "Noble Theatrical Agency."

"Larry Noble, please."

"One moment." Her voice clicked off and tinny music played in Sam's ear. He and Larry could still iron things out, Sam was thinking. Sure, there were all kinds of great possibilities out there. Commercials, for one thing. Anybody who was anybody did commercials, and they were a lot easier than doing a television show. His show might go into reruns, and that would mean residuals. Talk shows were always looking for interesting guests. Somebody important might be watching and his career would kick right back into high gear again. Damn, why couldn't everything be this easy?

"Hello?" The secretary was back on the line. "Mister Noble has gone to lunch with a Mister Buck Beaumont. If it's important, you can reach him at the Fish House."

Sam slammed the phone down.

He was back in the saddle again. The motorhome was loaded with provisions and with his reading glasses he could at least see where the hell he was going. He was feeling better already, even though he'd wasted half an hour and a pocket-ful of dimes making those stupid telephone calls. Ten cents for a telephone call! The telephone company was almost as money-hungry as his lawyer was.

Well, he had to call Howe, and now that was out of the way. He wanted to call Monica and he did, but as soon as he heard her voice he knew there was no use talking. He didn't have to call Larry, but he thought he did, and now he knew just where he stood with that big phony.

There was no use dwelling on the past. He just had to let it go. He was off on a big adventure and he needed his wits about him if he planned to get through it in one piece. So how about a little music and something to eat! Sam leaned forward and opened the paper bag Tina had given him. Inside was a crushed peanut butter and jelly sandwich, a Twinkie, and a hand-rolled cigarette. Sam started to throw the cigarette out the car win-dow, but changed his mind and stuck it under the owner's manual in the glove compartment. It might come in handy someday.

He took a bite of the sandwich and clicked on the radio.

"... Five men have been arrested for breaking into the of-fices of the Democratic National Committee in the Watergate office complex in Washington ..."

Sam turned to another station.

"... Beanball Berrigan is on the mound for the Red Sox, and the batter is Long Way Lonnigan, cleanup man for the White Sox. Berrigan looks again at Lonnigan, he's into the windup, there's the pitch, and Lonnigan is down. He'll go to first base, and that'll bring on Home Run Hannigan. What a spot for Berrigan. Bases loaded. Lonnigan at first, Finnegan at second, Mulligan at third. Berrigan into his windup, there's the pitch, and Hannigan is down ... "

Sam turned to another station.

"... the two convicts are identified as Stitch Mason and Louie 'The Blade' Salvatore. Warden Bilford Wormley says the men escaped by cutting through a fence at Four Walls Prison outside of Sacramento, California, and fleeing in a stolen car. Both men should be considered armed and extremely dangerous ..."

• • •

A black Ford Fairlane raced down Highway 95 east of Reno. The driver took a drag on his cigarette, then flipped it out the car window. If anyone had seen him do it, they wouldn't have said a word. The man's face was enough to scare a blind man. Hard steely eyes. Mouth turned down in a permanent frown. A pale white scar that zigged from his left ear and zagged all the way down to his collar.

His passenger was almost handsome, except for a large misshapen nose. He was studying a road map, and now he looked over at the driver. "Hey, Stitch," he sneered. "Slow down. All we need's a damn speeding ticket."

"Relax, Lou," Stitch answered. "I ain't seen a car on this road since we left Fallon."

"Yeah, but that don't mean nothing." Louie looked back at the map. "The way I figure, we stay on this road until we get to Vegas."

"And then what?"

Louie shrugged. "We get hold of some cash and hightail it to Mexico."

Stitch tried to grin as he eased up on the gas, but it came across as a grimace. "Mexico! Mariachis. Margaritas. Muchachas. *Mamacita!*"

"Well, just take it easy. We ain't there yet."

"See if you can get some news on the radio," Stitch said. "I like to hear my name on there."

Louie flipped on the radio, and music surged through the car.

"Chicken wings, and a bottle of gin
Chicken wings, and a bottle of gin

Chicken wings, and a bottle of gin
We're gonna have ourselves some fun tonight

We're gonna dance and sing
And stuff our face
With no regard for the human race

We're gonna eat those wings and drink that gin
Go out that door, then come back in
We're gonna have ourselves a real good time
Tonight."

Louie turned to another station.

"... President Nixon promises a complete investigation of the break-in at the Watergate complex in Washington by five men, who were arrested after ..."

Louie turned to another station.

"... in other news, the world's greatest poker players will be in Las Vegas in October for a five hundred thousand dollar winner-take-all poker tournament at Blackie's Casino. The tournament is expected to draw dozens of players and hundreds of spectators. Most of those spectators won't be there to see the game, but to view the half-million dollars in cash, which will be on display during the tournament."

Louie looked at Stitch. Stitch looked at Louie. Was this divine providence or what? All they had to do was waltz into this Blackie's joint, scoop up half a million bucks that was right there in plain sight, slip across the border, and they were home free.

In fact, their whole escape had been a breeze. It all started when Louie stole a spoon from the prison cafeteria. He sharpened the spoon handle at the tool shop, then over a course of three months he chiseled four blocks loose in the cell that he shared with Stitch. Stitch's job was to stand at the cell door and make sure none of the screws was making his rounds.

One night, while everyone was watching Sunday night football, they removed the blocks and wiggled their way out of the cell. They came out on a long corridor that led to the storage rooms. Then they jimmied open a window in one of the rooms, waited for the searchlight to sweep past, and raced to the fence. Using wire cutters they found in one of the storage rooms, they cut through the fence and finally found themselves outside the prison.

Their luck got even better after that. They found a light-blue Ford Fairlane in front of a dilapidated motel, and one of the car doors was unlocked. A rubber sign stuck on the driver's door read: ACE NOVELTY COMPANY. Stitch peeled it off while Louie hot-wired the ignition. They drove a few miles until they found an old pickup parked in a farm yard. Trading the truck's plates for those on the car, they hid out in an orchard until the sun came up. At dawn, they pried open the trunk and found a regular treasure trove.

There was a jug of water and a man's suitcase, with enough clothes for both of them. Now they would look like respectable businessmen instead of a couple of cons on the loose. Behind the spare tire, Louie found a small plastic box. He opened it and made the most important discovery of all. Inside was a gun! It looked like a 45-caliber revolver, with a big black barrel and a nice wooden handle. Louie tossed the box aside and held the gun almost reverently in his hands.

Meanwhile, Stitch was still rummaging through the trunk. "Look, Lou. Here's a can of spray paint."

"Give it here," Louie ordered. He stuck the gun in his waistband and began to spray black enamel over the car's surface.

"Waddaya doing that for?" Stitch cried.

"Think about it, Stitch. The guy who owns this car is going to report it stolen, right?"

"Yeah. So?"

"And the cops will be looking for a light-blue car, right?"

Stitch grinned. "Lou, you're a genius."

They monitored the car radio as they drove east through California, staying on back roads and living on fresh fruit and vegetables. The cops were searching for a light-blue Ford, and nobody gave them a second look. The only problem was keeping the car filled with gas, until Stitch found an old rubber hose in a dumpster at a rest area. That started a new routine. They would cruise into a little burg around midnight, look for a used-car lot, then siphon enough gasoline out of the cars to fill their tank again.

Now they had it all. Clothes, a getaway car, a gun, a rubber hose that was as good as a credit card, and most important of all: a plan. Five hundred thousand dollars was waiting for them in Vegas, and nobody better get in their way.

Sam found some music on the car radio just as he was coming into San Bernardino.

"Chicken wings, and a bottle of gin
Chicken wings, and a bottle of gin
Chicken wings, and a bottle of gin

We're gonna see the preacher man tonight
We're gonna say our vows
And exchange rings
Then tear into them chicken wings

We're gonna eat those wings and drink that gin
Go out that church, then come back in
We're gonna have ourselves a real good time
Tonight."

Sam glanced down at his speedometer; the needle was at eighty, and he was inside the city limits. He'd better slow this baby down. He touched the brake, but a black-and-white cruiser had already pulled up behind him. Then he heard a police siren and saw flashing lights in his sideview mirror. With a dull feeling of panic Sam swung off the road.

He sat there, drumming his fingers on the steering wheel. What should he do in a situation like this? Stay in the motor-

home and act surprised when the patrolman comes up? Say
something? Something like:

"Me? Speeding?"

"Sorry, Officer, I was just on my way to the garage to have
my speedometer fixed?"

"My baby's having a *wife*?"

No, that was no good. Maybe he should walk over to the
police car and—and do what? Tell him who he was? Apolo-
gize? Try to bribe him? No, that was no good, either. Besides,
it was too late. The patrolman was already outside Sam's window, taking off his sunglasses.

It was Clyde.

Clyde did a double-take when he saw Sam. "Well, fart in
church and call me Thursday," he exclaimed. "What the hell
are *you* doin' here?"

Sam tried to smile. "I'm just out for a ride, Clyde."

"You look different with glasses on. I liked you better the
other way."

"That really hurts my pride, Clyde."

"By the way, I clocked you at eighty-two point six," Clyde
clucked curtly.

"Well, I was trying to slow down when you stopped me. I
really tried, Clyde."

Clyde's hands were on his hips. "You know, speedin' is
the number-one cause of most major accidents."

"You're right. I've got no place to hide, Clyde."

Clyde's ticket book was out. "Well, seein' as how we're
old friends and all, I'm only gonna give you a warnin'. I gotta
at least do that."

"Okay, I suppose I can take that in stride, Clyde."

Clyde handed the book and pen to Sam. He scribbled his
name across the bottom.

Sam W~

Clyde tucked the ticket book in his back pocket. "Where you headin', anyways?"

"The way I'm driving, I might wind up at the Continental Divide, Clyde."

Clyde wiped his brow with his hand. "I wish to hell I was goin' somewheres. They got me workin' all over the dad-burned state."

"I could sure use a guide, Clyde."

"Well, this ain't a good time to be out drivin' around. A coupla convicts escaped from the penitentiary up at Four Walls. There's a A.P.B. out on 'em, so keep your doors locked and your windows up. Them guys could be anywheres."

"I'll keep my eyes pried, Clyde."

Clyde squinted at his watch. "Tell you what. I'm just about off duty. What say you treat me to a hamburger and a ice-cold root beer?"

"Sounds good. This heat's got me fried, Clyde."

"Follow me."

Clyde rolled past Sam's motorhome in his cruiser, spitting gravel all over Sam's windshield. Two miles down the highway Clyde slammed on his brakes and stopped in front of a restaurant. A sign, supported by yellow telephone poles, spelled out the word COPABANANA. A long line of people waited to get inside.

"By the time we get something to eat I could be in Las Vegas," Sam said to Clyde. Now why did he say Las Vegas? The words just popped into his head.

Clyde gave him a playful punch that almost doubled Sam over. "Give me your hands," he said. "I'll show you one of the advantages of bein' with the Highway Patrol."

Sam reluctantly put out his hands, and Clyde snapped his handcuffs tightly over Sam's wrists. He winced with pain as Clyde gave him a rough shove toward the entrance. "Step aside, folks!" he commanded in a loud voice. "I got a prisoner here."

The hostess led them to a table, keeping her distance from Sam. She dropped two menus on the table and hurried away. Meanwhile, Clyde laughed so hard his sunglasses fell off.

"How about taking these handcuffs off?" Sam asked. His hands were already turning blue.

"Yeah, yeah, okay," Clyde chuckled. He dug into his pocket and pulled out a small key. As he unlocked the handcuffs, the waitress appeared at their table. "Ready to order?" she asked Clyde.

"Hamburger and a ice-cold root beer."

"You want the regular, deluxe, king size, or jumbo hamburger?"

"Jumbo," Clyde answered, "and hold the onions." He looked over at Sam. "I got a date tonight," he explained.

"You want the regular, the large, the giant, or the humongous root beer?"

"The humongous, and don't cram it full of ice like you did last time."

The waitress eyed Sam suspiciously. "What's he going to have?" she asked Clyde.

"I'll have the same," Sam said.

Clyde watched the waitress walk away, then put away his handcuffs. "So where you from, Durango?" he asked, shifting comfortably in his chair.

"Texas," Sam answered, still rubbing his wrists. "I moved to California about twenty years ago."

"No shit? You're from Texas? Hell, I was raised there myself."

Sam didn't answer.

"So what part of Texas you from?" Clyde asked, leaning forward.

"Oh, a little town on the Gulf Coast called Gilbert. You probably never heard of it."

"GILBERT?" Clyde roared. People at the tables around them began to stare. "SON OF A BITCH, THAT'S WHERE I'M FROM!" People at the tables around them began to leave.

"Excuse me." The waitress appeared with their burgers. "I'll be right back with the root beers," she said. "I have to get someone to help me carry them."

Clyde's mouth bulged as he took a huge bite of his burger. "We're about the same age, so how come I don't remember you from school?"

"My real name was Duran. Sam Duran."

Clyde grinned broadly. "Sam Duran! Yeah, I remember now. You're the one they used to call the medicine man."

Sam cringed. It was true. Somewhere between his freshman and sophomore year, Sam's complexion went haywire. Some kids got pimples, others got acne. Sam got leprosy. He tried every cream, salve, and lotion on the market in an effort to clear up his complexion, and that's how he got his nickname.

Sam's father finally took him to a skin specialist. This was back when x-rays were used with wild abandon, chiefly on teenagers with bad skin. On his first visit, Sam was under one of those humming clacking machines for almost an hour, and when he left the clinic his face was bright red. His classmates had looked upon him with such morbid curiosity that he gave them the only excuse he could think of. "I was welding and I forgot to put my helmet on."

Now here he was in a restaurant shaped like a banana, chowing down on hamburgers with a cop named Clyde and talking about the good old days that in reality weren't good at all. On top of everything else, he didn't even remember Clyde. Neither the name nor the face jarred his memory. "Clyde, I'm sorry, but I just can't place you," he finally admitted.

"I was the school crossin' guard. Then I went in the army, in the M.P.'s. Then I was a security guard over at the mall in Whittier. And now I'm one of California's finest." He smiled lovingly at his badge, then looked back at Sam. "You ever been back to Gilbert?"

"Once. My dad died fifteen years ago and I went back for the funeral. I got there on a Monday, left on Tuesday. He was all the family I had."

"Sorry," Clyde said. Then his face brightened. "No wonder you wasn't at the class reunion."

"When was it?"

"Three months ago. I took all the sick pay I had comin', almost two weeks worth. Drove down there and put myself up at the new Holiday Inn out on Morton Road. Lived like a king. Even ordered breakfast from room service."

"Did you see anybody I might remember?" Sam asked.

"Hmm, let me see," Clyde frowned, looking off into space. "Do you remember Audrey Hickie?"

Sam sighed. He remembered Audrey, all right. She was the head cheerleader at Gilbert High, a scrumptious thing with legs right out of a negligee ad. They went horseback riding one autumn afternoon and wound up playing grab-ass under a mesquite tree. Sam managed to get her jeans off over her white buck shoes, but before he could get himself undressed he'd had a shuddering climax. The next morning Sam's complexion was as clear as a bell.

"What about Audrey Hickie?" he asked Clyde now.

"She was there. Remember how purty she used to be? Well, you wouldn't recognize her now. She weighs about three hunderd pounds and her hair's gone completely gray. About the color of yours."

Sam touched his new moustache self-consciously. "Clyde, tell me. Did my name come up at the reunion?"

Clyde frowned. "No. Then again, mine didn't come up either, and I was *there*. 'Course, no one probably recognized me with my uniform on."

"You wore your uniform to the class reunion?"

"Thems all I got is uniforms," Clyde grinned. "Hell, I ain't never had to wear nothin' else." By now Clyde's hamburger was gone, and he was using both hands to drag his root beer closer. "Hey, speakin' of Gilbert, remember the old school song? We sung it at the reunion, and it had everbody in tears." Clyde cleared his throat, then launched into the melody in a surprisingly soft sweet voice.

"G for Gilbert
I for Ilbet
L for Lbert, too
B for Bert and
E for Ert and
R for Rt and
T for T, too ..."

Sam joined in for the chorus. He was back in the basketball gym and the big homecoming game was only minutes away.

"If we ever leave dear Gilbert
Far from here to roam
It will be eternally
Our home, sweet home!"

Sam checked his watch, then climbed to his feet. "I'd better get going," he said to Clyde. "I'm on my way to Las Vegas." It was official now. For better or worse, Sam was headed for a new life in a new place.

Clyde gave him a wave then called to the waitress. He was ordering another hamburger.

Sam was back on the road, and soon San Bernardino gave way to sparse rolling hills. Somewhere up ahead was Las Vegas, although Sam knew in his heart that the glittering city was not his final destination. Someday he would find a small town with well-kept homes and shady streets, and people who smiled and said good morning. There would be a green grassy park with swings and picnic tables, and a crystal-clear lake jumping with catfish. The men would be big and rawboned, and the women would smell like freshly-baked pies. The air would be clean and pure, the children polite, and every day a holiday. There was a place like that somewhere, and Sam would find it. Someday.

A sign zipped past. "Victorville, 27 miles." He yawned and rubbed his eyes. Off the highway was a field, planted in neat rows of green. A rutted dirt road snaked down one side toward a stand of trees. It looked like the perfect place to spend the night. He slowed the motorhome and turned off the main highway.

He parked in a dark clearing underneath the trees. Birds whistled from branches overhead and the wind gently rustled in the trees. They were the same sounds Daniel Boone must have heard two centuries ago, and suddenly Sam's situation didn't seem so bad.

Although he was no outdoorsman, Sam knew how to build a campfire. At least he'd learned that much from doing a weekly television show about the old West. Dead tree branches and a few stray boards were scattered on the ground, with a pile of smooth white stones off beyond the trees. He gathered an armload of the stones, which he set in a circle. He stacked another load of stones on top of them, and laid twigs, branches, and boards inside. When the fire was going, he went inside the motorhome and got the chrome rack out of his oven. He propped it on top of the stones, then set his brand new coffee pot on top. While he waited for the water to boil, he sat with his back up against one of the trees, his arms behind his head.

Ah, this was the life. What he ought to do was find a little piece of land like this and settle down. Raise a family? No, he wasn't getting married again. Maybe more along the lines of a couple of dogs, and maybe a cat.

"DON'T MOVE, BOY!"

What the hell? Sam's left eye was staring into a big black tube, and Sam's right eye was staring into another black tube. Standing behind the double-barreled shotgun was the meanest-looking hombre Sam had ever come up against.

12

"Don't shoot!" Sam cried. "I'm unarmed!"

He heard the stranger breathing, air rattling in, air rattling out. Then the stranger spoke again, his voice low and gravelly.

"You are trespassing on private property, boy."

"I didn't know," Sam stammered. "I was just—just camping out for the night. I didn't see any signs. Listen, fella, you put that cannon down and I'm gone."

The stranger lowered his shotgun. "Do you realize where you are?" he growled.

"Uh, no. No *sir*."

"This here's sacred ground, boy. Those rocks over there mark the grave of Chief Soothing Breeze of the Cherokees. And you got a *fire* going on part of his tombstone."

Sam blew on the fire, but the flames rose higher. "I'm sorry," he said. "I'll put those rocks back right now. Hot or not. And thanks a lot."

"Hold it." The shotgun came up again. "You don't look like no graverobber to me. What's your name, anyway?"

"Sam Durango."

Down came the shotgun. "Sam Durango? The movie star?"

"TV star."

Up came the shotgun. "Okay! TV star."

"Yeah, and I might as well tell you the truth. I'm scoutin' locales for a new series. It's gonna be called—uh—'Injun Sam.'"

"I don't know," the stranger hesitated, lowering the shotgun. "You don't look like Sam Durango to me. What with those glasses and that piss-ant moustache."

"Yes, I'm Sam Durango," Sam insisted. "Look, I'll show you." He reached into his pocket for his billfold.

Up came the shotgun.

"Easy there," Sam said. "I was just going to show you my driver's license."

Down went the shotgun. The stranger studied Sam's license by the light of the fire and then passed it back. "I'll be danged! Sorry, Mister Durango, but a man can't be too careful nowadays, or ain't you been listening to the news?"

"News? What news?"

"Two convicts escaped from Four Walls a couple days ago. That's why I got so nervous when I saw your fire." The stranger's face darkened. "Say, maybe you better spend the night at the house."

"No, no, I'll be okay here," Sam said. "That is, if you don't mind."

"Well, all right, but put those rocks back in the morning. We don't need no evil spirits around here, especially right in the middle of watermelon season."

Sam took one more look at the stranger's shotgun. "Yeah, those watermelons look nice. Mighty nice."

The stranger dug out a stubby pencil and a wrinkled piece of paper. "Before I go, how about giving me your John Henry, Mister Durango? It would look damn good over my fireplace."

"Yeah, sure."

"There you go," Sam said.

"Thanks," the stranger said. "I'll put this one up with my other two auty-graphs. Much obliged."

"Who else you got?"

The stranger beamed proudly. "Franklin Delores Roosevelt and Buck Beaumont."

Buck Beaumont was going to haunt Sam forever.

Sam watched the fire until it crumbled to red glow and gray ash. The night was still and the moon was almost a full circle, casting long eerie shadows off Sam and the trees. Getting to his feet, he brushed at his clothing. He should have his head examined, leaving the comfort of a house on the beach and three gorgeous girls to go camping in somebody's sacred watermelon patch. Worse yet, there was a dead person buried somewhere in the vicinity of his barbecue pit!

Sam closed the curtains and locked the doors. Then he fluffed his new pillow and pulled his new blanket over him. But his eyes kept popping open, and sleep seemed a long way off. Quiet moments like this were meant to be shared, and without Monica he was so … alone.

He tried not to think about Monica, but here she came creeping into his mind again, and into his heart. He married her—oh, when was it? "Cactus Classics" had been on the air for three years, so it must have been about seven years ago. Sam never remembered their anniversary date. He always got it mixed up with the day his father died and the day Pearl Harbor was bombed.

Monica had been a Playboy pinup during her L.A. party days, then had settled into an acting career. She was making a guest appearance as a waitress in one of the segments of "Cactus Classics" when they first met. The scene called for Sam to walk in and sit down, and for Monica to come over and take his order. His line was:

"Bring back some fat back and two stacks of flapjacks."

TAKE ONE

"Bring back a hat rack and two sacks of six packs."

TAKE TWELVE
"Bring back a Big Mac and two racks of thumbtacks."

TAKE FORTY-ONE
"Bring back a black jack and two packs of Ex-Lax."

Sam finally finished the scene by saying, "Bring me two eggs over easy and some Canadian bacon."

By this time he and Monica were giving each other flirty looks on the set. On the last day of shooting, he finally got up the nerve to ask her out for dinner. Then she invited him to her apartment for a home-cooked meal. On their next date they took a boat ride to Catalina, and a week later an outdoor concert at the Hollywood Bowl. Then they went to a movie and ate popcorn out of the same box. At her door that night he made a pass at her. She slapped his face. He proposed. She accepted.

Seven years passed. Now it was all over, and for the life of him Sam couldn't figure out when everything fell apart. The newness between them wore off after awhile, but didn't that happen to everyone? His work at the studio didn't seem to interest her since she retired from acting, but—what the hell—it bored him, too. And maybe they didn't make love as often, but they were still comfortable around each other. They loved each other, trusted each other, believed in each other. At least, *he* thought they did.

If only they had sat down and talked about it. If only a light had gone off in his head that something was wrong. If only he could have seen it coming. Well, it probably wouldn't have made any difference. Their marriage just started to unravel, like an old blanket, and Sam—big fool that he was—never even noticed. By the time he knew anything was wrong it was too late, and now here he was sleeping by himself in a motorhome.

Seven years down the drain. Two thousand days, two thousand nights. Valentine's Days, and birthdays, and paydays, and rainy days. Silent nights, holy nights, little fights, and making up. Now all of Sam's hopes and dreams, the worrying and wondering, had collapsed into nothing more than a dusty pile of bitter memories.

He'd always suspected that one day he would wake up and Monica would be gone. He'd always wondered when the television gravy train would finally drop him at the station. He'd even dreamed about packing it up and starting over again. And now it was all happening. Well, he would face his future one day at a time. That's all he could do. Time was his enemy, but in a way time was his friend, too.

Sam woke with a start. Sunlight streamed through the window and for a moment he wasn't sure where he was. Then it all came back. He was in his motorhome. He'd spent the night under a little patch of trees somewhere outside of Las Vegas and gotten through it in one piece. Now he was hungry.

Sam lit a fire on his kitchen stove and started the coffee. Then he went to his refrigerator, retrieving a carton of eggs and a package of sausage. He hadn't known there was a refrigerator in his motorhome until he read his owner's manual. Thank God Curly didn't know that, or he would have nicked Sam for another thousand dollars.

He brought his breakfast to the small dining table. The food looked okay, although he'd accidentally busted both egg yolks and burned the sausage. He'd forgotten to buy bread so he didn't have any toast, which was just as well because he didn't have any butter or jam, either. He also forgot to buy salt and pepper, so he ate the eggs plain.

Then he washed everything in a sink of cold water and took a quick cold shower. There was no use going to all the trouble of lighting the hot water heater, because he was anxious to hit the road. The stranger with the shotgun might show up again.

That reminded Sam of the barbecue pit. He went outside

and gingerly felt several of the stones. They were cool to the touch. Working quickly, he carried them all back to where he found them the night before. Then he washed his hands and climbed into the driver's seat.

Sam pulled back onto the main highway and headed east. A black limousine was parked on the shoulder. Sam gave it a wide berth as he went past and turned on the car radio.

"... Meanwhile, a search continues throughout the West for escaped convicts Stitch Mason and Louie 'The Blade' Salvatore, who escaped from Four Walls several days ago. They are believed to be driving a stolen light-blue Ford Fairlane, California license number ATU-757. Mason is serving a life sentence for kidnapping and armed robbery. Salvatore is serving life for the attempted murder of a federal judge. The two men ..."

Sam turned the radio down. The black limousine had pulled back onto the highway and seemed to be following him. Sam slowed down, waiting to see what the car would do. Finally it swung out and roared past him. Sam almost laughed with relief. He'd been making too many westerns.

He cranked his window down, and air swooshed into the car like heavy syrup. Cars and trucks buzzed past him. They reminded Sam of angry little bumblebees, everyone in a hurry except him. Heck, he had his whole life to get where he was going.

Glancing at his face in the rearview mirror, he noticed that his moustache was not quite as straggly today. His hair was grayer, too. He looked more rugged, more down-to-earth, more ... well, older.

He'd only had a moustache once, and that one was fake. It was for one of the episodes of "Cactus Classics." The show was written by grade school students as a class project and was given a nationwide publicity campaign before being shown. It finished sixty-seventh in the Nielsen ratings.

He was jolted back to reality by the sight of the black limousine again. Now it was parked off the pavement and a man standing next to it waved frantically as Sam started to pass. The man was short, with slicked-down black hair. Black must have been the man's favorite color because he was wearing a black shirt, black suit, and black shoes. The only break in the color was a white tie, knotted around the man's neck like an exclamation point.

Sam rarely picked up hitchhikers, especially with two escaped convicts on the loose. But this one seemed harmless enough. Besides, Sam needed someone to talk to. He was spending too much time thinking about himself, and about the past. It would be good to hear someone else's viewpoint for a change.

He hit the brake and pulled off the highway. The man ran to the motorhome, while Sam poised his foot over the gas pedal. If the guy was wearing an earring, Sam would leave him in the dust right now.

"Thanks for stopping, buddy," the man said as he climbed into the passenger seat. "I had some car trouble."

"Glad to help." Sam put the motorhome in "Drive" and started off again. There was no use volunteering to look at the man's engine. The only thing he knew about cars was where the gasoline went.

The man wiped his face with a black handkerchief, giving Sam a curious look in between swipes. "So, how far are you going?" he asked finally.

"Las Vegas," Sam answered. "Kind of blowing with the wind, you might say."

"Vacation, huh? Sounds like fun. As a matter of fact, that's where I'm headed." He poked a hand in Sam's direction. "My name's Vinnie. Vinnie Despuchi."

"Mister Rescuchi," Sam acknowledged, shaking his hand.

"Despuchi."

"Desnuchi."

"Despuchi! Aw, hell, just call me Vinnie."

"Vinnie."

"So—what's your name?"

"Sam Durang—er, Duran. Sammy Duran." Well, he wasn't lying. He used to be Sam Duran, and maybe it was time he started using that name again. He was tired of being Sam Durango, tired of all the looks and all the questions.

"Good to meet you, Sammy," Vinnie said. "Hey, you mind if I take my coat off? The damn thing's stuck to my back." Vinnie wriggled out of his black jacket and laid it carefully over the back of the seat. He wore a black silk shirt, and on both sleeves were his initials in a fancy-scripted monogram.

Vinnie loosened his tie, then turned back to Sam. "So, Sammy, have you ever been to Vegas before?"

"Once." Sam had gone there with Monica on their first anniversary. He lost a few dollars in the slot machines, but Monica won it all back. She lined up three stars on one of the machines, and suddenly lights flashed and sirens went off. Sam thought the place was being raided, but it was just Monica winning twenty-five dollars. Damn! There was Monica, in his head again. To distract himself, he asked Vinnie, "How about you?"

"I live there," Vinnie laughed.

"Oh? What do you do?"

"I run a casino." Vinnie leaned toward Sam. "In fact, I could use a guy like you."

Sam was speechless. He was being offered a job in Las Vegas! A week ago, he was the star of his own television show with a beautiful wife and a high-powered agent and a big house up in the Hollywood hills. Now he was on his way to Las Vegas in a motorhome, sitting next to a complete stranger who wanted to put him to work in a casino!

"What would I be doing, Vinnie?" he asked. "I don't know anything about gambling."

"I can teach you everything you need to know by the time we get to Vegas."

That didn't sound too encouraging to Sam.

"I own a place called Blackie's," Vinnie went on. "It's real class all the way. Nice carpet, chandeliers, velvet wallpaper. Nothing like those joints where I used to work, back in Chicago."

"Chicago," Sam repeated absently. "I played the Coliseum there once."

"Huh?"

"I mean … I paid a dollar to see 'em there once," Sam stumbled. Damn it, he had to quit being Sam Durango.

"To see who?"

"Chicago. You know, the—musical group."

"Yeah? Well, I still go back there once a year. To see the boys."

"Oh, you've got family there?"

"About the biggest most important family in the Midwest," Vinnie boasted proudly.

"Hey, that's great," Sam smiled warmly. Vinnie probably took his boys camping and fishing, all the things Sam would do if he had children of his own.

A few small stores and isolated farmhouses slipped past, then Sam and Vinnie were in Victorville. Sam slowed the motorhome, searching for a garage, but Vinnie waved his hand. "Forget it, Sammy. I'll send somebody out to get the car. Hey, you got any beer in here?"

"In the refrigerator. And get me a Coke, will yuh?" Sam smiled to himself. Vinnie had just offered him a job, and here was Sam dishing out the orders.

"Listen, Vinnie, about Las Vegas. Exactly what would I be doing there?"

Vinnie opened his beer and took a long swig. Then he unwrapped a fat cigar, bit off the tip, and lit up. "First things first. Vegas is all on the up and up nowadays. Gambling's controlled by the state. You don't have a record, do you?"

"Nope, never made one," Sam replied with a smile.

"You never did any time in the slammer?"

"Slammer?"

"You know, the can."

"About five minutes every morning." He'd like to hear Vinnie ask Buck Beaumont that question.

Vinnie chuckled. "Okay, you're clean. Good. Now here's the situation. I need dealers, and I was thinking I might use you on one of the crap tables."

Sam frowned. "You want me to be a dealer on a *crap* table?" No wonder Vinnie asked him about the can.

"Hey, it's easy. In fact, all gambling games are easy. If they were complicated, nobody'd ever play anything, and I'd be out of a job."

"Well, darn, Vinnie, I've never even *seen* a crap table. I wouldn't know what to do."

"Look, it's real simple. You give the shooter the dice, okay?"

"Okay." So far it sounded all right.

"If the shooter rolls a two, three, or twelve, he loses. If he rolls a seven or eleven, he wins. If he rolls a four, five, six, eight, nine, or ten, that becomes his point and he has to roll that number again before he rolls another seven. If he does, he wins. If he rolls a seven first, he loses. See? I told you it was simple. Kids play this game in the street, back in Chicago."

Sam made a face. "I don't know, Vinnie. Maybe I could just drive you around in the motorhome."

"I'll start you out at forty bucks a day plus meals, and you'll probably make another sixty a day in tokes. What do you say?"

"Sixty Cokes a day?"

"Tokes! That's what dealers call tips."

"Why?"

"I don't know, Sammy. They just do." Vinnie stubbed out his cigar in the ashtray. "Do you need a place to stay when we hit Vegas? I can fix you up with a room at the hotel till you get on your feet."

"Does Blackie's have a parking lot?"

"Sure, with trees and everything."

"That's good enough for me, Vinnie. I've got my room right here."

"So you do," Vinnie smiled. "One thing, though. You're going to need some clothes. Black shirts, black slacks, black shoes. We furnish the white ties and aprons."

"Aprons?"

"All the dealers wear aprons. It's house policy."

"Why?"

"Well, it keeps everybody honest," Vinnie explained. "A casino is like a bank, Sammy, and we've got to take the same precautions."

"Oh." Maybe if Sam turned around right now, he could be back at the beach house by nightfall.

"That's why when you get off the game you always clap your hands," Vinnie said.

"Come on," Sam laughed. "You're kidding me, right?"

"I never kid about business, kid. You clap your hands once and turn 'em face up. That shows the boxman you're not stealing anything."

"Boxman?" Sam echoed wearily.

"Yeah, he's the one who watches the game."

"Oh, so he's the boss."

"I'm the boss. The boxman works for me."

"Oh, so the boxman watches the game and you watch the boxman."

"No, the floorman watches the boxman."

"Oh, and who watches the floorman?"

"The pit boss."

"Who watches the pit boss?"

"The eye in the sky."

"Eye in the sky?"

"That's the man upstairs."

"You mean—God?" Sam whispered, fighting an urge to genuflect.

"No, no, NO! The man upstairs over the casino. We've got two-way mirrors in the ceiling, and that's where our eye in the sky is. He watches everybody."

All this was too much for Sam. Boxmen and foremen and pit bulls and pie in the sky. He was beginning to wish he'd left Vinnie Cuhoochi standing on the side of the road back by his black limousine.

"There she is," Vinnie said suddenly, waving expansively toward the windshield.

Sam peered through the glass. Down below he could see lights of every color twinkling in the distance. After a hundred miles of sand and cactus, it looked like the bejeweled necklace of some giant goddess, flung carelessly across the sand.

Sam's arms began to tingle and his breath came out in short ragged bursts. This was the place Lady Luck called home, and he was going there to join her. Valerie's voice rang in his ears, "Las Vegas, that's the town for a guy like you. Las Vegas."

The buildings loomed closer now and a sign zipped by.

"Welcome to Fabulous Las Vegas." Then came the hotels, one after the other. HACIENDA. TROPICANA. DUNES. CAESARS PALACE. FLAMINGO. SANDS. DESERT INN. RIVIERA.

Famous names blinked from every marquee. The Mills Brothers. The Smothers Brothers. The Ames Brothers. The Everly Brothers. The Righteous Brothers. The Doobie Brothers.

Off to the left Sam saw a massive whitewashed building with a white canopy and white banners flying. Huge letters across the top spelled out the word WHITEY'S. In front was a tall neon sign. IN PERSON. BETTY WHITE. BARRY WHITE. WHITEY FORD. Underneath the names, in smaller print: White Russians 50¢.

Directly across the street was an enormous black building with a black-tiled entranceway and black plate-glass windows. A large sign read BLACKIE'S, and underneath it was a lighted marquee. IN PERSON. KAREN BLACK. SHIRLEY TEMPLE BLACK. BLACK SABBATH. In smaller print: Black Russians 49¢.

"Pull up in front," Vinnie said, tightening his tie and slipping on his jacket.

Sam stopped the motorhome at the front entrance. A doorman in a black uniform ambled over, but when he saw Vinnie in the front seat he snapped to attention. "Mister Dee!" he exclaimed, rushing to open Vinnie's door.

Vinnie got out, then turned to Sam. "Thanks, Sammy. Follow the parking lot around back. There's a nice spot out by the golf course where you can stay. I'll square it with security. Get yourself some clothes and see me tomorrow morning at ten o'clock."

Sam followed Vinnie's directions and came to a parking lot next to a cyclone fence. On the other side of the fence was the golf course. The lush patch of green, with sparkling blue pools of water here and there, looked strangely out of place in the middle of the desert and the gaudy casinos. A few gnarled trees hung over the fence, and Sam parked his motorhome underneath one.

Then he locked the motorhome and started back to the hotel. The same doorman saw him coming and ran to open the front door. "Thanks," Sam said, starting to feel like a television star again. "Say, is there a men's clothing store in here?"

"Yes sir!" the doorman barked. Then, in a confidential tone, he added, "But you don't want to buy anything in the hotel. Prices are sky high."

Sam stopped. "Well, is there any other place around here?"

"Try Satchmo's. It's half a block down the Strip, next to Luigi's. You can't miss it."

"Thanks again," Sam smiled warmly. His faith in humanity was slowly being restored.

"And ask for Julie," the doorman said. "He's my cousin."

Sam joined a slow-moving crowd on the sidewalk. The warm evening air felt good on his skin, nothing like the muggy heat of Los Angeles, and for the first time he could remember there were stars in the sky. For the first time he could remember, there was *sky*.

He reached Luigi's, which turned out to be a small diner. A sign in the window caught his eye. "T-Bone and Fries: $1." Sam swallowed. He hadn't eaten anything since breakfast and was starting to feel a little weak in the knees. The waitress gave him a bored smile as he went inside. "Grab a seat, honey," she said, handing him a greasy menu. "I'll be with you in a minute."

The diner was so small that Sam could hear every conversation. A man two tables away gave the waitress his order. "Scrambled eggs and ham."

She hollered across the room to the cook. "Pair of sailors, shipwreck 'em, and throw 'em in the pig pen!"

A woman ordered raisin toast and a glass of milk.

"Bugs on bread, burn 'em, and squeeze an albino!"

Now she was at another table and bellowing more orders to the cook.

"Beached whale and a side of hay!"

"Submarine with a screen door!"

"Shoot one and castrate it!"

Then she was at Sam's table. "What'll it be, honey?"

"I'll have the T-bone and fries."

"How you want it?"

"Well-done."

"Burn a heifer and give it the shingles!" she hollered.

Suddenly Sam wasn't very hungry. "Excuse me," he called after the waitress. "I've changed my mind. Just bring me a jelly doughnut and half a cup of weak coffee."

"SCRATCH THE HEIFER, GIMME A COW PIE, PUNCH A HOLE IN IT, SQUIRT IT AND HURT IT, SHIMMY UP A BEAN TREE, BREAK IT IN HALF, AND SPIT IN IT!"

Sam got back to the motorhome around midnight, his arms loaded with packages. Whistling softly, he unpinned the new garments and stacked them on top of the table. Then he scratched his head. Where the heck was he going to put everything? He opened his small closet and looked inside. Hanging there were his Western coats, his Western pants, his big-buckled belts, and his string ties.

He took everything out of the closet and crammed it all into the empty shopping bags. They would go in the trash tomorrow. The only thing he kept was a tan suit with curly brown embroidery, and a brown and orange shirt with little silver corner-pieces on the collar tips. He folded these carefully and slid them into an overhead storage compartment. They were his favorites, and he couldn't bear to part with them.

Then into the closet went all his new clothes. Blue jeans, white shirt, brown slacks, tennis shoes, knit shirt with an alligator over the pocket, sweater, sports coat, bathrobe—and, of course, black slacks, black shirts, and black shoes.

He'd better get to bed. This was the beginning of a new life, and he didn't want to start it by oversleeping. He switched off the lights and closed the curtains. Then he slipped out of his clothes and crawled into bed, his mind spinning like a top.

He was starting a brand new job tomorrow, but he wasn't

exactly sure what kind of job it was. It had something to do with dealing crap. Well, hell, he'd been dealing crap all his life; maybe it was time he got paid for it. Let's see, what did Vinnie tell him? If the shooter rolled a seven on the first roll, he won. If he rolled an eleven, he lost. If he rolled a two, three, or twelve, that became his point, and he had to roll that number again before he rolled a four, five, six, eight, nine, or ten. No, wait a minute, that didn't make sense. Actually, *none* of it made sense. Well, he'd worry about it in the morning. Right now he had to get some sleep. He closed his eyes and rolled over on his side.

Suddenly, someone banged on the door, and the sounds reverberated through the metal motorhome like rifle shots. Sam sat up so quickly he thumped his head on the ceiling. Mumbling to himself, he flipped on a light and edged cautiously to the door. All he could see outside the window glass was a dark silhouette. Who could be beating on his door at one o'clock in the morning? Sam slipped on his new robe, the price tag still hanging from a sleeve, and put on his reading glasses. Then he unlatched the door and swung it open. Standing there with a flashlight in his hand was Clyde.

14

Sam stood dumbfounded at the door. "What the hell are you doing *here*, Clyde?"

The man with the flashlight looked at him blankly. "My name's Ron. I'm a security officer with Blackie's Casino."

"Oh, sorry," Sam said, taking a closer look. He could see now that the uniform had thrown him for a loop. "I thought you were a—friend of mine."

"No, I'm Ron Hartley. Security. Blackie's Casino."

"Yeah, I got that. Well, what can I do for you, Ron?"

"You're camping on private property. This lot's for hotel guests only."

Here we go with that private-property stuff again, Sam thought, but at least Ron wasn't packing a double-barreled shotgun. "Ron, I've got permission to park here. It was supposed to have been cleared with you guys by Vinnie Parduchi."

"Who?"

"Vinnie Parduchi. He owns the place."

"You mean Vincent Despuchi?"

"Yeah, that's him."

Ron eyed Sam doubtfully, then fumbled his walkie-talkie out of his Sam Browne belt. "Chief, this is two-fourteen. I'm in the east parking lot. Some fella is camped out here in a motorhome."

A blast of squawk and static came out of the walkie-talkie, but Ron seemed to understand every bit of it. The noise stopped abruptly, and Ron pushed the talk button again. "Yes sir, well, he says he got permission to park here from Mister Despuchi." More squawks and static, then Ron turned to Sam. "What's your name, sir?"

"Sam Durang—er, Sammy Duran."

"Says his name is Sammy Duran, sir." After a final blast of squawk and static, Ron slid the walkie-talkie back into his Sam Browne. "Sorry, Mister Duran," he said with a shrug. "I didn't know."

"Aw, it's okay. Just don't shoot me with your high beam." Ron grinned. "You mean my flashlight?"

Sam nodded and Ron threw back his head, braying with laughter. "Haw haw! That's a good one, Mister Duran! That's a darn good one."

"And don't call me Mister Duran. The name's Sammy."

"Glad to meet you, Sammy. I'm Ron Hartley. Security. Blackie's—"

"Blackie's Casino. I know."

Suddenly the walkie-talkie blasted to life again and Ron listened intently to more squawks and static. "Ten four," he replied into the mike, then turned again to Sam. "The Chief says he has a message for you. You're supposed to go down to the Clark County Sheriff's Office in the morning and get a sheriff's card. You can't work in a casino without one."

"Oh. Okay."

Ron hitched up his pants. "So you're going to be working at Blackie's, huh?"

"Yeah, Mister Coohoochi gave me a job dealing crap."

"That's great. Maybe I'll see you around." Ron turned to leave, then stopped. "Could I ask you something, Sammy?"

"Sure."

"For a guy who's not even sure how to pronounce the boss's name, how'd you get permission to park here? And how in the world did you get a job at Blackie's?"

"Mister Guhnoochi was hitchhiking, and I gave him a ride."

"Haw haw!" Ron brayed with laughter again. "That's a

good one, Sammy. That's a darn good one."

The Clark County Sheriff's Office was located in an old brick building downtown. Trying to parallel park the motorhome was beyond Sam's driving skills, so he stopped on a residential side street, then walked eight blocks to the downtown area. Fremont Street was crowded with casinos, bars, and souvenir shops. It was nothing like the Las Vegas Strip, where glittering resorts were set back from the road like palatial Southern mansions.

He went inside the sheriff's office and took a number. Half an hour later his number was called by a prim young man wearing horn-rimmed glasses and a bright orange tie. A nameplate on his desk identified him as A. D. Pranger.

"Name, please?" Pranger asked, not looking up.

"Duran. Sammy Duran."

"Nevada resident?"

"Yes."

"I need to see some identification."

"Driver's license okay?"

"Anything with your name and address on it."

Pranger took Sam's driver's license and studied it. Then he stared at Sam, his eyebrows furrowed and his lips puckered. "It says here your name is Sam Durango and you live in California."

"Well, here's the deal. My real name is Samuel Duran. I changed it to Sam Durango. Now I'm changing it back, only I'm changing it to Sammy Duran instead of Samuel Duran."

Pranger snorted noisily. "You can't just change your name willy nilly like that. It has to be done legally." Pranger began to write on Sam's application, reading out loud as he wrote. "Sam Du-rang-o." He looked up. "Like the movie star?"

"TV star."

"Uh huh." He began writing again. "A.k.a. Samuel Duran, a.k.a. Sammy Duran. Resident of California."

"Nevada," Sam said. "I moved here yesterday. I just haven't changed things yet."

"Okay, but be sure that you do. You've got ten days. Local address?"

"Blackie's Casino."

"Room number?"

"Uh, parking lot."

Pranger sat back. "Parking lot?"

"I'm living in a motorhome."

"Oh." Pranger looked back down at Sam's application. "Well, we're just about done here. That'll be thirty-five dollars."

Sam handed the money across the desk.

"A couple more questions, then we'll get your photo and fingerprints."

"Is all this really necessary?"

"Certainly. It's to protect the casino industry from infiltration by organized crime, that sort of thing."

And the thirty-five dollar fee multiplied by ten thousand casino workers didn't hurt either, Sam thought. "I see."

"Now then. Have you ever been arrested?"

"Of course not. Er, wait a minute. Yeah, once. I was arrested once."

"I mean, since you've been an adult," Pranger laughed.

"Well, yeah. Once."

The pencil was poised over Sam's application again. "Charges?"

"Uh, suspicion of—armed robbery."

"Wow."

"It's a long story, but the charges were dropped."

"Anything else?"

"Uh, possession of a—controlled substance."

"Oh boy."

"Charges were dropped!"

Pranger scowled at Sam as he shoved the application over to him. "Sign this," he said.

Sam scribbled his name across the bottom.

An hour later Sam hiked to his motorhome, a laminated sheriff's card tucked away in his wallet where thirty-five dollars used to be. He followed Las Vegas Boulevard back to the parking lot at Blackie's, then headed for the casino, feeling stiff and starchy in his black uniform and shirt. If things worked out, he might buy himself a car. Whenever he drove somewhere in the motorhome, everything inside either rattled or fell over. And damn, just look at the time. It was already a quarter after one, and he was supposed to meet Vinnie Conduchi at ten o'clock.

Sam got directions to Vinnie's office, which was up a carpeted stairway on the second floor. A secretary looked up as Sam entered the room. She appeared to be in her mid-seventies, with coal black hair piled atop her head in an old-fashioned beehive. "Can I help you?"

"Yes, I have a ten o'clock appointment with Mister Eldoochi."

"You mean Mister Despuchi?"

"Yes."

The secretary glanced at her watch, then back at Sam. "Your name, please?"

"Sammy Duran."

"Oh! Mister Despuchi is in a meeting, but he said to tell you to go down to the sheriff's office and get your sheriff's card. You can't work in a casino without one."

"I know. That's why I'm late. I just got it."

"That's fine. Now you've got to go to Personnel and get processed. They'll give you your uniform, your name tag, and everything else you'll need. You won't actually start working until tomorrow."

"Great!" Another day without dealing crap was fine with Sam. He found the Personnel office in a dingy building behind the casino, and spent two hours filling out his employment application. There were a lot of tricky questions. Next of kin. Sam left that one blank. Present address. Another blank. Telephone number. Blank. Car. Yes. License number. No. Sheriff's card. YES! Previous employment. Pioneer Studios. Dates worked. June, 1962, until one week ago. References. That was a tough one. He certainly couldn't write down Monica, or Jay Cohen, or Larry Noble, or Buck Beaumont, or Valerie. Damn, he didn't even know her last name. He walked over to the woman behind the counter. "What's the owner's name?" he asked her.

"Vincent Despuchi."

"How do you spell that?"

"D-e-s-p-u-c-h-i."

"Thanks." Sam wrote Vinnie's name down under References. Then he wrote it again on a slip of paper and stuck it in his pocket. He wouldn't ever forget Vinnie's last name again.

After he turned in his job application, Sam got a white tie and apron and a name tag with SAMMY printed on it in bold white letters. He also got a meal card, which he was told to present each time he ate in the hotel coffee shop. He could eat anything on the menu, except steaks, chops, beef, pork, prime rib, seafood, or poultry. That was fine with Sam. He needed to lose a little weight anyway.

On his way out of the hotel he saw a small barber shop. The barber was reading a newspaper. "DRAGNET FOR CONS EXPANDS," the headline read. "Haircut?" the barber asked, getting to his feet.

"Yeah," Sam said, easing into the barber's chair.

"How do you want it?" the barber asked.

"Short."

"Yes, sir."

Sam watched himself in the mirror as the barber clipped away. He'd worn his hair long ever since he'd been an actor.

Now, with a new job and facing the public, it wouldn't hurt to look as neat as possible. Besides, the shorter hair and moustache and reading glasses changed his whole appearance. He'd never be recognized as Sam Durango now. Maybe Ernest Hemingway, but definitely not Sam Durango.

"All done," the barber announced, flapping Sam's sheet with a crack. "That'll be forty dollars."

"Forty dollars for a haircut?"

"You're a guest in the hotel, aren't you?"

"No, I work here."

"Well, why didn't you say so? Three dollars."

Sam strolled down the sidewalk. He could have cut across the hotel property to the motorhome, but he felt like getting some exercise. He went past Luigi's and Satchmo's, past a Quik Foto shop, a liquor store, a souvenir stand, then found himself in front of a pawn shop. A bored man wearing a green eyeshade studied Sam quietly as he walked inside.

"Can I help you, Mac?" he asked.

"Maybe."

"Well, we're not buying any jewelry right now. No watches, rings, silverware. No guns, cameras, sporting equipment, car radios, stereos, televisions—"

"I'm not selling," Sam said. "I'm buying."

"Oh! Well then, you've come to the right place, sir. We've got a great selection of watches, rings, silverware, guns, cameras, sporting equipment, car radios, stereos, televisions—"

"Television! I need a television set."

"I've got some real beauties. Here, look at this seventeen-inch color console. It sold brand new six years ago for six hundred, but I can let you have it for two ninety-five."

"No, it's too big. What have you got in a small portable?"

"Well … here's a thirteen-inch black and white rabbit ear for thirty bucks. Couple of the knobs are missing, but it still works."

"It's fine. I'll take it."

The man shrugged as he carried the small TV set to the

counter. "Thirty dollars, plus tax. That comes to thirty dollars and ninety cents."

Sam pulled out his wallet. Damn, all he had were two tens and four wrinkled singles. He took out his five thousand dollar cashier's check. "Can you change this?"

"Mister," the man said, taking the check from Sam, "I can change the spots on a pair of dice." He disappeared into the back and came out carrying a cardboard box. "Sorry, we're out of hundreds. I had to give you all tens and twenties."

Sam got back to the motorhome just as it was getting dark. He plugged in the small television, turned on the set with a pair of pliers, and the image of a newscaster blurred into view on the screen. Then he opened the cardboard box, gazing down at the biggest stack of money he'd ever seen in his life. It was too late to go to the bank, so he decided to stash the money. But where? A cabinet would be too obvious. That's the first place a burglar would look. Inside the stove? No, he might forget the money was in there and wind up having soufflé dinero for dinner one night. Refrigerator? Hell, why not? There was nothing in there but a carton of eggs, some soft drinks, and a six-pack.

After he finished stacking the money inside the refrigerator, Sam opened a can of chicken-noodle soup. When it was hot, he brought it to the table and began eating it right out of the pot. His attention was on the television newscaster.

"In other news, a police dragnet has been expanded from California to the Canadian and Mexican borders for escaped convicts Stitch Mason and Louie 'The Blade' Salvatore. The two escaped from Four Walls late last week, and are believed to be driving a light-blue Ford Fairlane."

Mug shots of the two men appeared on the screen. Mason looked like five miles of bad road, with a white flumed scar running from his left ear to just under his chin. His eyes were as cold as ice, and his mouth was turned down at the corners in a permanent frown. By contrast, Salvatore was almost handsome, with dark oily hair and brooding black eyes. The only thing that spoiled his appearance was a huge misshapen nose that looked like it had been broken with a baseball bat.

"Sightings of Mason and Salvatore have been reported in Texas, Kentucky, North Dakota, Maryland, and the Florida Keys. These have all been cases of mistaken identity, however, and have done nothing more than lead authorities on a wild goose chase. In fact, earlier today a woman in Harrisburg, Pennsylvania, turned in her own husband and brother-in-law."

Woman on TV: "Well, my husband sure looks like this Salvuh-torry guy. And he never comes straight home from work, like he's hiding something, you know?"

Shaking his head, Sam slurped the last of his soup. It was a damn wonder that Monica hadn't put the finger on *him*. "Police headquarters? Yes, that convict you're looking for is hiding out in a motorhome in the parking lot of Blackie's Casino in Las Vegas." Hell, she probably would have done it if she'd known where he was. He could picture it so clearly. Cops surrounding his motorhome with their bulletproof vests on and their guns drawn, one of them edging to the door while the others took cover behind their squad cars. Then—

Blam!

Blam!

Blam!

Someone was pounding on the door. Sam turned down the television, then peered through the window glass. Son of a gun, it was Ron, the security guard. "Come on in," Sam said, opening the door.

"Thanks," Ron grinned, setting a sack on the table. "I brought you something to eat."

"I just finished a bowl of soup."

"Hell, soup's just an appetizer. Come on, eat a hamburger. I brought four of them. Two for you, two for me."

"Thanks," Sam smiled. "How much do I owe you?"

"You don't owe me anything. I got them from the coffee shop on my meal card."

"Well, okay, but at least let me get you something to drink."

"A Coke would be good. Where are they? I'll get them."

"They're in the refrig—oh! Never mind. I'm already up." Sam sprang to his feet and hurried to the refrigerator. Pushing a stack of ten dollar bills aside, he got out two Cokes and brought them to the table.

"Did you get your sheriff's card?" Ron asked as Sam bit into his burger.

"Mmph, yup."

"Did you get processed?"

"Mmph, yup."

"You'll like working at Blackie's," Ron said. "Everybody's like family here. Heck, some of the people even call the owner Uncle Vinnie. Not me, though. I call him Mister Despuchi."

"Yeah. Well, Blackie's is all the family I've got right now, so I guess I'll fit right in."

Ron brayed with laughter. "Haw haw! That's a good one, Sammy! A darn good one."

Sam finished his first burger, then reluctantly opened the wrapper on the second. "Let me ask you something, Ron."

"Shoot."

"How come you guys only carry flashlights? Aren't you allowed to carry guns?"

"Nope."

"What if something happens? You know, like what if those two convicts show up in the casino some night?" he asked, taking a tiny bite.

"What convicts?"

"Those convicts who escaped from Four Walls. It's been all over the radio and in the newspapers."

"Didn't hear about it."

"No? Well, it just seems to me that if you're supposed to be protecting the place, you ought to be allowed to carry a gun."

Ron took a long swig of his Coke. "We used to carry guns. Then one night a couple of bozos robbed a guy in his hotel room.

They locked him in the john when they left, but they didn't know there was a phone in there. So the guy gets on the bathroom phone and calls security. And this trigger-happy security guard—he doesn't work here anymore—pulls out his gun and starts firing at them when they get off the elevator. Bullets were flying everywhere. It's a darn wonder nobody got killed."

"Gosh."

"And right after that, Mister Despuchi said no more guns."

"So now all you've got is a flashlight?"

"And a two-way radio. And a set of handcuffs. It works out okay. We call the cops if anything really serious happens. Besides, I don't really know if I could shoot somebody anyway. Could you?"

Sam shrugged. "I've shot a few men in my life."

Ron grinned. "Yeah? How many?"

"Oh, about fifty."

Ron brayed with laughter. When he stopped, Sam leaned forward. "Ron, can you keep a secret?"

"Sure."

"I did shoot fifty men, but it was only make-believe. You see, I used to be on TV."

"Uh huh," Ron eyed him suspiciously.

"I was in a show called—"

Suddenly Ron's walkie-talkie went off and a barrage of static and noise blared through the motorhome. Ron listened intently, then got to his feet. "Got to get," he said to Sam. "Old Gert is sticking slugs in the slot machines again. See you at work."

Sam waved goodbye and cleared the table, tossing half of his second burger into the trash. He couldn't believe how much he'd eaten. Worse, he'd almost told Ron that he was Sam Durango. Here he was, under an assumed name and more or less wearing a disguise, and he nearly spilled the whole thing to someone he hardly knew, just because that person brought him a couple of burgers that he didn't even want.

Oh well, live and learn. Tomorrow was another day. In

fact, tomorrow was the big day. It wouldn't hurt to go over that game of crap again. What was it Vinnie told him? Four, five, six, eight, nine, or ten was a winner on the first roll. Two, three, or twelve were losers. Eleven was a tie. Seven was a winner if the shooter had a number, but seven was a loser if the shooter didn't have a number. Or was it that eleven was a winner and seven was a loser? Oh, to hell with it. He'd find out for sure tomorrow. The worst thing they could do was fire him, and he wasn't even sure he had a job yet.

Blam!

Blam!

Blam!

Ron must have forgotten his flashlight or walkie-talkie. Sam swung the door open, and there stood Vinnie Sarduchi!

"Vinnie!" Sam exclaimed.

"Hi, Sammy," Vinnie said, sweeping past Sam and dropping a sack on the table. "I thought you might be too shy to use your meal card before you actually started working, so I brought you a couple of hamburgers from the coffee shop."

Sam's stomach skedaddled sideways.

"And I'm going to sit right here and make sure you eat every single bite."

15

A black Ford Fairlane rolled down the Las Vegas Strip. Stitch Mason turned and grinned at his passenger. "What a place, huh, Lou?"

"Yeah," Louie answered, buffing his pistol with his coat sleeve. "I was here a few years ago when I was dating that stripper broad. Only problem was I couldn't keep her away from the one-armed bandits."

"One-armed bandits?" Stitch scratched his head. "How'd they make a living, Lou?"

"They weren't *people*, Stitch. They were slot machines."

"Can I play one, Lou? If I can crack a safe, I can crack a slot machine."

"We ain't here for no vacation. Now shaddup and drive. I'll tell you where to stop."

Soon the Las Vegas Strip was behind them, the glittering casinos replaced by sparse vegetation, vacant warehouses, and seedy motels. In front of one was a half-lit neon sign: "PALM SPRINGS MOTEL. Rooms $5 a Nite. No Fone, No Pool, No Pets, No TV, No Maid Service, No Credit Cards."

"Pull in here," Louie ordered.

Stitch took a drag on his cigarette, then flipped it out the car window. "How come you wanna stop here, Lou? We gonna heist the place?"

"No, we ain't heisting the place, Stitch! This is gonna be our home for awhile."

Stitch was reading the sign in front of the motel. "Palm ... Springs ... Motel ... Rooms ... Five ... Dollars." He turned to Lou. "Can we afford a nice place like this?"

Louie dug into his pocket and came out with a wad of wrinkled bills and a handful of change. "Well, let's see how much we got. Ten dollars from that drunk we rolled in Tonopah. Four dollars in quarters out of the Coke machine in Gabbs. Three-eighty from the recycling plant in Fallon for all them aluminum cans we picked up. So yeah, we're okay. We got about eighteen bucks."

Stitch was figuring out loud. "Eighteen into five goes three, carry the three, multiply by five, subtract three. We got enough to stay here for ... eight days!"

"How'd you ever get out of reform school?" Louie sneered. "We'll be broke by the end of the week if we stay in this dump. But it beats sleeping in the car. Come on, let's check it out."

Their room consisted of two sagging beds, a dusty night stand, and a cracked window with a broken shade that looked out onto a deserted parking lot. The toilet was at the end of a dark hall and, from appearances, looked like it had been used by everyone in Clark County. The place was a dump, all right, but for two cons on the loose it was the perfect hideout.

Outside their room was a dented garbage can with no lid. Lou chased flies away and started sorting through the rubbish.

"Did you lose something, Lou?"

"Shaddup! You'd be surprised what you can find in garbage cans."

Out came a crumpled stack of stained visitor guides. "Look at these, Stitch," he grinned.

"Yeah? So?"

"Coupons! Get it? Free coupons! Here's one for a free buffet. We can get some decent food and it ain't gonna cost us a cent. Here's another one for free cocktails. And look! Here's a whole bunch of coupons for free souvenirs!"

It was ingenious! All they had to do was stroll into the casinos with a handful of coupons and they'd never have to work again. It sure beat making license plates in the machine shop at Four Walls.

Then Stitch came up with a good idea for once in his life. Eyeing a plastic beer mug they redeemed at Blackie's, he said, "Hey, this may be a piece of crap, Lou, but I bet we could sell it to some lame-brained tourist for a coupla bucks."

It worked like a charm. They set up a small stand on the Strip and sold everything they scrounged from the casinos: key chains, baseball caps, ashtrays, T-shirts, change cups, empty cocktail glasses, gaming guides, playing cards. It kept them in enough money to pay the daily tab on their motel bill.

To find out how the search for them was progressing, they read old discarded newspapers. The story of their escape from Four Walls slowly went from page one to page seven to out of the papers completely. But there was another story Louie was looking for, and he finally found it in the local section.

Plans for Poker Tournament Finalized

Vincent Despuchi, owner of Blackie's Casino, has announced that plans for the casino's $500,000 poker tournament have been finalized. The tournament, to be held October 31, will pit the world's top poker players in a winner-take-all contest of five-card draw. Entry fee for each contestant is $25,000. Despuchi said that the tournament, with the prize money on display, will coincide with the casino's special Halloween celebration. "This should attract nationwide attention to Las Vegas," Despuchi said. "We expect a record crowd of spectators for this event."

Louie grinned as he finished the article. "Hey, Stitch!" he said. "We been invited to a party!"

• • •

Sam's first day in the casino was a terrifying experience. Making movies and television shows was kid stuff compared to the non-stop tension of slot machines ringing and people screaming and dice flying and piles of bills changing hands.

Sam arrived at the casino shortly before ten o'clock, his short gray hair neatly combed and his gray moustache starting to fill in nicely. Vinnie was waiting for him near the crap table, and introduced him to the other members of his dice crew. The three, all short with slicked-down black hair, were identified by name tags as Vito, Carlo, and Gino.

Without so much as a nod to Sam, the three dealers started toward the table. Sam trailed along behind them, Vinnie at his side. "Now listen," Vinnie said to him. "Just do what the others do. If the other dealer pays everyone, then you pay everyone. If the other dealer picks up everyone's money, you pick up everyone's money. If something else comes up and you're not sure what to do, just ask the boxman. He'll tell you. Okay?"

"I think so."

"Don't worry, Sammy. You're gonna do just fine."

A game was already underway at the table, and Sam was told to replace the stickman. Stickman? Vinnie didn't tell him anything about any stickman. To his dismay, Sam saw that the stickman was the person who gave the dice to the shooter and called out the numbers when they rolled.

After the first roll, Sam tried to bring the dice back to the center of the table and raked his stick right through everybody's chips. On the next roll, he accidentally poked a woman behind him with the end of his stick, and she kicked him in the leg. Then the shooter proceeded to throw both dice off the table, and Sam left to look for them. Some guy in a dark suit grabbed him and led him back to the dice table, kicking Sam in the other leg.

The whole day went like that. "This place shouldn't be called Blackie's," he told Vito, Carlo, and Gino at the end of his shift. "It ought to be called Blackie's and *Bluey's*."

"Hey, you did great," Vito said.

"Yeah," Carlo chimed in. "You made a few mistakes, but so what? Everybody makes mistakes."

"Here's your tokes," Gino said, handing Sam a wad of bills. "Your cut's seventy-two dollars."

"Thanks," Sam said, gingerly taking the money. "Thanks a lot!"

"We're going to have a drink at the bar," Vito said. "Wanna join us?"

"No, thanks," Sam said. This was one of those rare instances when Sam didn't feel like drinking. He just wanted to get back to the motorhome and lie down. Maybe there was a can of band-aids in there somewhere.

Sam shut the door of his motorhome and took off his black uniform. Then he went to the refrigerator and tossed the paper bills inside. Damn, he would have to get to the bank one of these days.

Closing the curtains, he stretched out on the bed. He was tired, and his feet hurt and his legs ached, and every time he closed his eyes he was back in that damn casino again. Of course, most of the players were as intimidated by being there as he was, so no one really gave him a hard time. As far as the payoffs went, Sam had worked out his own formula for that. Whenever he paid off a winning bet, he just kept piling on the chips until the player smiled. Then he would take one back. He was right every time.

So all in all, he'd done okay. It would be nice to tell another person about it, to share his day's experiences with someone close. Sam hadn't lived all alone for a long time, and the motorhome seemed so empty. If Monica were here, he would have her in stitches. Knocking chips over, getting kicked in the leg, making almost a hundred dollars with no idea how he did it. Then again, Monica would probably just smile and say, "That's nice." She never really listened to him; that was the problem. And just what was she doing in his thoughts again anyway? Valerie was the one he missed the most. Why hadn't he written down her phone number? Of course, there were other ways to get in touch with her. He could write her a letter, for one thing, or send her a telegram. He knew her address.

The trouble was that Sam wasn't much of a writer. It was hard enough for him to *say* what was on his mind, let alone try to put his thoughts down on paper. Once Larry Noble had suggested that he write his autobiography, which sounded scary to Sam. Autobiographies were usually written by people right before they died. Larry insisted it would be a big hit and boost his career, so finally Sam bought himself a portable typewriter and set it up in the guest bedroom. He named his autobiography "The Durango Fandango," (which took half the day) and started on chapter one. By now it was 2:30 p.m.

"I grew up in Texas." 3:15 p.m. "I moved to California." 4:00 p.m. "I became an actor." 4:30 p.m. "I acted in several movies, and then I acted on television." 5:05 p.m. He wadded the paper into a ball and threw it into the wastebasket. Then he put the typewriter back inside the case and carried it to the dark confines of his closet, never to use it again.

Now here he was living inside a tin can in the middle of the desert with his life savings in the refrigerator, and the only thing he knew for sure was that he'd never go hungry. Not as long as there were hamburgers in the coffee shop at Blackie's.

Sam's eyes were heavy, but he was starting to get an idea. He would get a couple of days off soon. He'd drive to California and see Valerie. They'd spend a night together. It sounded good! But shouldn't he let her know he was coming first? What if she wasn't there? What if she had a date with somebody else? What if she didn't want to see him again? He'd better think about this some more.

Sam's breathing slowed, and then the world's oldest crap dealer fell asleep.

It was Sam's second week on his new job. He'd just finished his shift and was walking through the coffee shop. He
saw an empty chair in the employee section and sat down.
Across the table was a girl with long blonde hair and big red
eyeglasses.

"Sam?"

Suddenly the world came to a crashing stop. The room was
frozen in time, like a strip of film in an old movie projector. All
the people around them were suspended in motion, and the
only noise in the room was Sam's heart. Ker blap, ker blap, ker
blappety blap.

"Valerie?" he whispered.

She nodded brightly and the world came back to life. People
began to move and talk again, but all Sam saw was Valerie.

"I didn't recognize you for a minute," she was saying. "You
look different with glasses on."

"Uh, yeah, I—I can't believe it! Valerie, what are you doing here? I just left you in California!"

She laughed, and to Sam it was like ice-cold champagne
rippling down a mountainside. "I work here," she said simply.

"What about the—what about the club? What about Teeny
and Gildee?" The words tumbled out of his mouth like dusty
marbles.

She laughed again. More champagne. "The club got closed

for selling booze after hours. Tina's working up a nightclub act. And Gilda moved in with a guy in San Diego."

Sam sat back in his chair. God, she was gorgeous, and it was so good to see her. She wore a flimsy black uniform that dipped low in front and it was hard for Sam to keep his eyes focused. All he wanted to do was hold her in his arms and never let go.

"I missed you, Sam."

"You did?" he exclaimed, wide-eyed. "I missed you too, Valerie. I almost drove to California to see you. God, I can't believe you're actually here. How did you wind up in Las Vegas, of all places?"

"I called a friend of mine and he hired me. And guess what I'm doing?"

Sam looked at her scanty outfit. "Dancer?"

"Nope."

"Prancer?"

"Nope."

"Blitzen?"

"No, Sam! I'm a cocktail waitress!"

"That's great."

She toyed with her plate of cottage cheese and pineapple. "I'll never forget the day you left," she said softly. "You were so brave. Off to see the world in your little motor house."

"Yeah," Sam said, remembering. "Come to think about it, you're the one who gave me the idea."

"Me?"

"To come to Las Vegas. Then I met Vinnie Kapuchi, and here I am dealing crap at Blackie's."

She frowned. "I don't know anyone by that name. The only Vinnie I know is Uncle Vinnie. Er, you know, Vinnie Despuchi."

"That's the one. I never can get his name right. I even wrote it down, but I can't read my damn handwriting."

She giggled. "Well, at least you haven't lost your sense of humor. This is my first day on the job and I'm afraid I haven't had much to laugh about." She touched his hand. "At least, not until now."

"When did you get here?" Sam asked, watching with dismay as she rose to her feet.

"Yesterday."

"Do you have a place to stay?"

"Yes," she answered, "but you can walk me to the parking lot."

Sam followed Valerie out the side door of the casino, and in a few moments they were at her car. Sam got in with her and directed her back to the golf course where his motorhome was parked, dark and foreboding, up against the cyclone fence.

She stopped, but left the engine running. "One drink," he pleaded.

"Well … all right."

He helped her into the motorhome and she followed quietly as he pointed out his little bathroom and his little stove and his little table. It was the first time she'd been inside and he found himself wishing she would never leave.

"Say," he said suddenly. "Why don't I get a little fire going outside? I'll make us a pot of real coffee, just like the pioneers used to make it."

"Okay," she said. "I'll get the cups."

Sam took his new flashlight and searched along the fence for firewood. He managed to collect several pieces of scrap wood, some pine cones, one broken tree limb that he'd have to push into the fire a foot at a time, and three golf balls. He also found an old newspaper stuck in the fence that he used to get the fire started.

Making a mental note to buy a couple of folding chairs, he brought a blanket from the motorhome and spread it out near the fire. Hypnotic flames danced in the darkness, and the burning wood snapped and crackled noisily. Sam stretched out on the blanket, gazing up at the stars a million miles away.

"Here you go," Valerie said, bringing two cups to the fire. "I made coffee on the stove. Try it."

Sam sat up and took a cup. "Mm, this is good! How come it doesn't taste like this when I make it?"

"Because I put bourbon in it," Valerie said.

Sam laughed. Working at Blackie's, he saw a lot of beautiful women, with their furs and their diamonds and their evening gowns. But they scared him. In fact, all women scared him. The divorce hanging over his head had dried up something inside him. He wasn't sure he could trust another woman. Not now, maybe not ever. But Valerie was different.

She finished her coffee and lit a cigarette. "Let me have one of those," Sam said. He lit it with a wooden match, gazing into her eyes as he smoked.

"She must have hurt you very much," she said softly.

"Who?"

"Monica."

"Why do you say that? Does it show that much?" Wait a minute, Sam thought suddenly. How did she know about Monica? He'd never mentioned her to Valerie.

"I heard you say her name in your sleep one night," she said quickly, as though reading his mind.

"Oh." His eyes went back to his cigarette.

There was a lull in the conversation while Sam pushed the tree branch farther into the fire. Valerie sat huddled on the blanket and he moved to her side, putting his arm around her.

She leaned her head on his shoulder. "So have you made any friends since you've been here?" she asked.

"Yeah, I have. Gino and Carlo. And Vito. They're on my crap crew. And I met a security guard named Ron. And Vinnie, of course. He's been real nice to me."

"No girls?"

"No. Except for you."

"Good," she smiled. Then she yawned. "I've got to go, Sam. See you tomorrow?"

"You bet." He reluctantly followed her to her car. "How about dinner tomorrow night? I get off at six."

"Okay," she said, tiptoeing to kiss his cheek. He fought the urge to crush her to him, to feel her body against his, to lock the door and set the alarm clock for February. But it was too late. She was gone. He watched her taillights until they were swallowed by the darkness. Then he stamped out the fire and walked to the motorhome, all alone again.

Sam was exhausted by the end of his shift the following day. A young woman had rolled the dice for two hours at Sam's crap table, and when the hand ended she got more applause than the president after a State of the Union message. But when he saw Valerie waiting for him in the coffee shop, suddenly his strength surged back. Her blonde hair was pulled to one side, a red ribbon holding it gently in place. Dangling red earrings framed her face like little wineglasses, and her uniform had been replaced with a pale pink sweater and tight black skirt.

"Are you hungry?" he asked. "Or do you just want to neck all night?"

"I'm famished. How does Chinese sound?"

"You're driving."

They left the hotel and Valerie turned off the glittering Strip onto a side street. She stopped in front of a small restaurant and Sam opened his door.

"Sam? Why don't you take off your name tag?"

"Hey, that's right."

"And your tie."

"Good idea."

"And your apron."

"That too?"

A petite hostess dressed in a flowered kimono led them to a small table in the corner. Sam opened his menu, only to find that it was printed in Chinese. "This is like trying to read the Hong Kong phone book," he sighed.

"Don't worry. A girl at work said to order the jumbo prawns in black bean sauce. She says it's delicious."

"Fine," Sam said. The waitress was hovering over them. "Shrimp and beans," he ordered. She placed two dainty cups and a pot of steaming tea on the table, then left.

Valerie smiled at Sam. "How was work?"

"Hectic. But it was worth it. I made a hundred and twelve dollars in jokes."

"Jokes?"

"Er, you know, tips. The guys call 'em jokes."

"Sam, they're called tokes."

"What would I do without you?"

"A funny thing happened to me today," Valerie said, pouring them each a cup of tea.

"What?"

"Oh, this millionaire from Oklahoma made a pass at me."

"He did *what?*"

"Well, he didn't actually make a pass at me. He just asked me to go out with him, that's all."

"And what'd you do?"

"I told him I was married."

Sam frowned. "You know, that's what I hate about you working in a casino. Guys see you in that dinky little outfit and the next thing you know they're panting like hyenas in a sandstorm. Maybe you oughta be a bookkeeper, or something."

"Oh, Sam, don't be ridiculous."

"Well, what would you do if some millionaire from Oklahoma made a pass at me?"

"I'd hit him over the head with my purse."

"I didn't mean a—" Sam sputtered. "I meant a—" Sam couldn't finish. Valerie was laughing her champagne laugh. Then he was laughing. They didn't even notice their food was on the table.

When they finished their meal, the waitress brought to the table a small silver tray with two fortune cookies. Valerie cracked one open and withdrew a small slip of paper. She read the words to herself, then smiled contentedly.

Sam waited. "Well, what's it say?"

She pursed her lips. "It says, 'You will meet a person who will show you the way to much happiness. Your future together stretches into the infinite, and Confucius will insure that your years be long and fruitful.'"

"Nice," Sam said. "Let's see what old Confucius has in store for me." He snapped his cookie into two pieces. Half the paper was stuck in one piece, and the other half was in the opposite piece. He carefully moved the slips of paper together.

"What does yours say?" Valerie asked.

Sam didn't answer. His message was:

DO NOT BUY ANYTHING ON TIME

A week later, Sam and Valerie both got the same day off. She packed a lunch and they drove to nearby Lake Mead for a picnic. Sam's contribution was a coat hanger for the marsh-mallows and three bottles of wine. They spent a lazy after-noon walking barefoot along the water's edge, holding hands, and watching high-powered boats churn across the lake.

By the time they returned to her apartment it was dark. Sam didn't know whether it was all the wine he drank or the magic of a perfect day, but as soon as she turned off the engine he took her in his arms. He kissed her long and tenderly, her mouth tasting like a field of flowers, and then his lips were on her throat. He could feel her swallow as he lightly let his fin-gers roam across her arms, edging closer and closer to her breasts ... three inches away, two inches, one, none. He was half-expecting a karate chop to his jugular vein, but instead she sighed softly. "Want to spend the night, Sam?"

Then he was in Valerie's bedroom. "I'll be right back," she said, quietly closing the bedroom door.

Sam glanced around the room as he unbuttoned his shirt, but his attention was riveted to the bed. It seemed to be breath-ing, rising and falling as though it were alive, and he won-dered for an instant if he was meant to be some kind of human sacrifice. He gingerly touched one corner of it. Son of a gun, it was one of those newfangled water beds.

He peeled off his clothes and pulled back the soft furry bedspread, revealing slippery satin sheets underneath. He crawled between them as the bed gently rocked and caressed him, and then a big wave came up and shot him halfway across the mattress. He came to a stop next to a small console with three knobs built into the headboard. He turned the first knob, and the water beneath him seemed to get warmer. He turned the second one, and the mattress began to shake and quiver. He turned the third knob. Suddenly he could hear rain and thunder all around him.

The bedroom door opened and there stood Valerie, wearing only her big red eyeglasses. Sam couldn't move. He just lay there between silken sheets, watching in an almost hypnotic trance as she walked slowly toward him, her figure silhouetted by a shaft of light from the hallway. There was just her, just him, just this one beautiful moment.

BRRRING!

The telephone rang.

"Let it ring," Sam breathed huskily. He couldn't tear his eyes from her.

"Answer it, Sam. It might be important."

Damn. Sam groped for the phone, still looking at her. "Hullo," he grunted into the mouthpiece.

"Valerie? It's Joan at Blackie's. One of the cocktail waitresses on swing called in sick tonight, and I was wondering if you could cover for her."

"Well, if it's really important—"

"You sound terrible, Valerie. Listen, forget it, I'll get somebody else. You just get yourself to bed right now. And drink plenty of fluids."

"Who was it?" Valerie asked as Sam set the phone down.

"It was Joan at Blackie's. She said to get yourself to bed right now."

17

Sam's divorce from Monica was final. He had called Howe and passed on his new address. Sam Durango, care of Sammy Duran, care of Golf Course, care of Blackie's Casino, Las Vegas, Nevada. All the official papers came back, and Sam read them carefully. He knew that the moment he put his signature on that divorce decree he was signing away most of his life, and most of everything he'd accumulated. But there was a whole new life ahead of him, and sometimes you just had to let the past go.

Sam Durango

Now he was free as an eagle. Free of Monica. Free of his house in Hollywood, and his sports car, and his chunk of land in Palm Springs. He was an eagle all right, but not a golden eagle. Bald eagle was more like it.

Sam was happy, though. He didn't mind being Sammy Duran or dealing crap at Blackie's. In fact, he liked living in the desert and being himself for a change instead of some chrome-plated cowboy. Just as important, Valerie liked him for what he was, not for what he used to be, and that was a big worry off his mind.

Now here it was October. Brashy flashy October, the time when there were no promises and no rewards. Another year was winding down, and October said, "So what?" Sam was sitting at the dining table in his shorts, watching through the window of the motorhome as workers changed the marquee in front of the hotel.

MASQUERADE PARTY FRIDAY
WEAR A COSTUME AND GET FREE DRINKS
$500,000 POKER TOURN A

"Fore!" he heard someone call from far away, then there was a knock on the door. "Come in!" Sam called absently, checking himself to make sure nothing was sticking out.

No one answered. Sam got up and opened the door. All he found was a black golf ball resting on his welcome mat.

"Hey, Sammy!" someone yelled.

Son of a gun, it was Vinnie Spaduchi! He was standing on the fairway, separated from Sam by the cyclone fence. "You're on the ball!" Vinnie cried.

"Thank you!" Sam hollered back.

"I mean, you're on *my* ball! Throw it back, will you?"

Sam picked up the ball and tossed it over the fence to Vinnie.

Vinnie caught it with one hand. "Thanks," he said, walking toward the fence. "Say, are you off today?"

"Yeah."

"How about playing a few holes?"

Sam shook his head. "I've never played golf before, Vinnie. I probably couldn't even hit the ball."

"Aw, throw some clothes on and get over here. The exercise will do you good."

Sam sighed. "Okay. I'll be right over."

He dressed, then joined Vinnie on the golf course. "Come on," Vinnie said to Sam. "We'll start at the next tee."

They stood at the edge of a long fairway. Off in the distance Sam saw a red flag fluttering in the breeze. "That's where you want to hit the ball," Vinnie said, getting a tee from his golf bag and punching it into the ground. He placed a ball on top of it, and handed a club to Sam.

"Stand over the ball. Bend your knees a little. Keep your head down. That's it. Now take the club back. Keep your arms straight. Don't try to kill the ball. Just give the club a nice— little—swing. There!"

Sam looked up, but didn't see the ball anywhere. "Where'd it go?" he asked Vinnie.

"Where'd it go? It's on the damn green!" Vinnie exclaimed. "That was one of the best shots I've ever seen!"

Sam's ball had landed twenty-five feet from the hole. He waited next to it until Vinnie got to the green three shots later. "Okay, now what do I do?"

Vinnie handed Sam a putter. "Stand over the ball. Keep your arms straight. Bend those knees a little. There. Now give it a nice little tap."

The ball rolled across the green and into the cup.

"Great shot!" Vinnie exclaimed. "You got an eagle!"

"An eagle? Where?"

"You got a two on a par-four hole. That's called an eagle."

"Oh, okay. Is that good?"

Sam and Vinnie finished playing two hours later. Sam wound up with two eagles, four birdies, two pars, and a nineteen on the last hole—where his ball either went into the sand or the water. It just didn't make sense to Sam that someone would go to all the expense of building a nice golf course, then leave sand traps and water holes all over the place. It ruined everything.

"Nice game, Sammy," Vinnie said, slapping him on the back. "Let's go to the clubhouse."

They sat down at a table and Vinnie ordered a round of drinks, signing for them with a flourish of his pen. "You know, Sammy, you could turn pro if you played this game enough."

"I don't think so. If it hadn't been for you, I'd still be trying to get off that first—uh—tee thing."

Vinnie laughed. "So how's everything else going?"

"Great. I like my job. And I'm seeing someone."

"I know."

"Yeah, I guess it's no secret, huh? She's a cocktail waitress. Her name's Valerie."

"She's a sweetheart. I love her. I always have," Vinnie said, or so Sam thought. The words were drowned out by a bartender blending ice for a margarita.

Then he heard himself say, "I'm in love with her."

"Have you told her?"

"No. In fact, this is the first time I've even said it out loud."

"Do yourself a favor, Sammy, and tell her how you feel. Life's too short to waste any of it. Take it from an old man who's been down the road a lot farther than you have."

"Oh, come on, Vinnie. You're not that old."

"How old do you think I am?"

"I don't know. Sixty-one?"

Vinnie laughed. "I'm seventy-nine years old. And I've been running casinos ever since Dewey was president."

"Well, golf agrees with you then, or something does. Because you look great, Vinnie."

"I enjoy life, Sammy. I try to cram as much into each moment as I can. And when I get too old to ride one horse, then I just get on another one."

"What do you mean?"

Vinnie stared quietly into his drink, as though looking into a crystal ball. "I'm getting too old for this business, Sammy. I'm putting the casino up for sale. Next month."

"What?" Sam swallowed.

"Five million dollars. You interested?"

Sam's mind began to tumble. Let's see. He had around eight thousand dollars in his refrigerator, and he was getting another sixty thousand dollars from Monica in January. He could sell the motorhome for maybe twelve thousand, so that gave him a grand total of—eighty thousand. Five million less eighty thousand came to—four million nine hundred twenty-thousand dollars. Damn.

"Vinnie, I couldn't come up with five million dollars if my life depended on it."

Vinnie chuckled. "You don't understand, Sammy. You don't have to come up with the whole five million. Ten percent down and you pay the rest out of your profits."

Sam's mind was tumbling again. Let's see. Ten percent of five million was five hundred thousand dollars, less his eighty thousand, which left a balance of—four hundred twenty-thousand dollars. Damn.

"Think about it, Sammy. Right now I've got to get back to the office."

"What's going on, anyway?" Sam asked, following Vinnie out the door. "The hotel marquee says something about a masquerade party."

"Oh, we're having a Halloween party Friday. All the employees are going to wear costumes, and we're capping the whole thing off with a big high-stakes poker tournament. Top prize is half a million bucks."

Vinnie turned to Sam as the limousine driver opened the car door. "Hop in, Sammy. I'll give you a ride."

Sam settled into the plush leather seat, then turned to Vinnie. "Could you have the driver stop at a phone booth? I want to call Valerie and see if she's coming by after work."

Vinnie opened a burled walnut cabinet. "Use this one."

"Thanks," Sam said, punching out the numbers on the phone pad. "Now if I just had another drink, I'd be all set," he laughed.

Vinnie opened another burled walnut cabinet. "Bourbon and water?"

"Thanks," Sam said. "Now if I could just hop in a steaming jacuzzi, I'd never ask for another thing."

Vinnie opened a burled walnut cabinet.

Just as Sam got back to the motorhome, Valerie pulled up in her car. He waved. She waved back.

"I brought you some dinner," she smiled.

"Great, I'm starved. What are we having?"

"Hamburgers from the coffee shop."

Sam's stomach seesawed savagely.

• • •

The doorman at Blackie's greeted guests with a warm smile. "Good afternoon, sir!" "Welcome to Blackie's, ma'am!" "Hello, folks, how are you?" Suddenly his face blanched. Two unsavory characters were approaching the entrance. This could be trouble.

One of the men had a white flumed scar running from his left ear to just under his chin. His eyes were as cold as ice, and his mouth was turned down at the corners in a permanent frown. The other man, with dark oily hair and brooding black eyes, had a huge misshapen nose that looked like it had been broken with a baseball bat.

"Er, welcome to Blackie," the doorman stammered, then moved out of the way.

The two men ignored him and walked inside. Louie rubbed his hands together feverishly while Stitch looked around in awe. "Are we gonna play the machines, Lou? Let's play the machines. Gimme some money and we'll play the machines."

"Forget the machines," Louie growled. "This is where they're having the poker tournament. We gotta case the joint."

The casino was an architectural nightmare, with hallways going in every direction and narrow aisles crowded with slow-moving groups of tourists. Signs overhead pointed every which way, but a pall of cigarette smoke nearly obliterated the neon words.

"Hell, the tournament'll be over by the time we get through this mob," Louie sneered.

"I could call in a bomb threat," Stitch said. "You got a dime?"

Just then Louie spotted a tall security guard standing nearby. "Let's ask this guy."

"He's a screw, Lou!"

"He's a rent-a-cop! He probably don't know what day it is. Come on."

The security guard looked in their direction as they approached. "Can I help you fellas?" he asked politely.

Louie peered at the man's ID tag. "Yeah, Ron. We heard something about a half-million dollar poker tournament they're having here, and we was wondering if you could tell us where it's gonna be at."

"Sure thing," the security guard said, pointing to his left. "Take that hallway past the coffee shop, turn right at the keno lounge, go past the gift shop and the showroom, and then take a quick left just past the elevators to the card room. You can't miss it."

"Uh, excuse me," Stitch chimed. "Is the half-million dollars in there yet?"

The security guard brayed with laughter. "Haw haw! That's a good one, sir. A darn good one!"

It was overcast and gloomy. The sky was a greasy gray, and lightning flashed in the distance. Sam hurried across the parking lot into the casino. All the employees in the coffee shop were talking excitedly about the masquerade party and the costumes they would wear on Halloween. Well, Sam wasn't going to be wearing any costume. He'd been wearing costumes in Hollywood practically all his life and he wouldn't do it again. Besides, Sam thought as he finished his bowl of Trix cereal and milk, Halloween was for kids!

"And you get suspended for two days if you don't wear a costume," one of the dealers was saying.

Well, wearing a costume might be fun at that, Sam decided. And he could go as—a cowboy! He even had his cowboy clothes stashed away in the motorhome.

Valerie walked into the coffee shop, dressed in her black cocktail waitress outfit. Sam could feel his heart beating faster. "Hi," she said, sitting across from him.

"Hi," Sam answered, his eyes going all soft and funny.

"I guess you heard about the masquerade party."

"Yeah."

"And the poker tournament?"

"Yeah."

"I'm going to be serving cocktails at the tournament."

"Do poker players drink a lot?"

"I don't know. But it costs twenty-five thousand dollars to

get in, so you know they've got lots of money."

"Well, exactly how does this tournament work, anyway? Each person puts up twenty-five thousand and then what?"

"The way it was explained to me is that they just keep playing until there's only one person left, and he gets the money."

"Half a million buckaroos," Sam said, shaking his head.

"Yes, and the money is going to be right there in the poker room so everybody can see it. Isn't it exciting?"

"I'll say!" he said, looking again at her skimpy outfit. The tournament was the last thing on his mind.

Suddenly the overhead lights dimmed, then brightened again.

"It looks like that storm's getting worse," Valerie said. "Maybe I better stay at your motor house tonight."

Sam was hoping it wouldn't rain. No, he wanted it to snow!

By the time Sam got off work the rain was falling in big heavy drops. He'd read somewhere that Las Vegas got four inches of rain a year. Judging from the gray skies overhead, the whole four inches was coming down tonight. Then his heart skipped a beat. Valerie's car was parked in front of the motorhome. With a grin, he walked to the driver's door and tapped lightly on the glass.

"Hello, Sam," Valerie said, rolling down her window.

"Hi, Sam!" someone called from the passenger seat.

Sam looked closer. "Tina!" he exclaimed. "What are you doing here?"

"It's a long story," Valerie muttered. "Let's go inside."

Tina was decked out in a sparkling green dress and green high-heeled shoes. And son of a gun, Sam thought with a smile, she was wearing her boobs tonight. He helped her up the steps into the motorhome, then came back down for Valerie.

"I can manage, Sam," she said curtly.

Tina chattered at the table while Sam hunted in the kitchen for refreshments. He returned with two Cokes, a bottle of bourbon, two mismatched water glasses, and a clean jar with a mayonnaise label still stuck to it.

"So what brings you to our fair city?" he asked Tina, pouring a shot of bourbon into the jar and taking a sip.

"I've got a gig at Whitey's," she announced proudly. "I finally hit the big time."

"Why, that's wonderful," Sam grinned. "Isn't that wonderful, Valerie?"

"Yes, it's wonderful."

"I called Valerie as soon as I got to town. Then she told me you were here, and I just had to stop by and say hello. Isn't this just wonderful?"

"Wonderful!" Sam agreed.

"Wonderful," Valerie muttered.

"So is that why you're all gussied up?" Sam asked.

"Yes. In fact, I've got a show to do in less than an hour." Tina leaned forward. "Why don't you two come? It'll be fun."

Valerie glared at Sam, then turned to Tina. "Tell Sam who else is in the show."

"Oh! Buck Beaumont! He's the one who hired me."

"Buck Beaumont!" Sam sat down heavily next to Valerie.

"It was the craziest thing," Tina babbled. "I was reading the newspaper and there was this ad for a nightclub singer. I called the number, Buck set up an audition, and here I am."

Sam tried to smile. "Why, that's—"

"Wonderful," Valerie finished for him.

"What's the matter?" Tina asked, looking from Valerie to Sam.

Sam sighed. "Nothing. It's just that Buck and I don't get along that well anymore. I don't know if it would be a good idea for me to go. But Valerie can."

"I'm not going, Sam."

"Why not?"

"I've got to work on my costume for the masquerade party."

"That's not until Friday," Sam protested. "You've got plenty of time to do that."

"Sam, I'm not going!"

Sam's eyes went wide in surprise. He'd never seen Valerie get so angry and it scared him. Hell, if anyone should be dodging Buck Beaumont, it was Sam. Why should Valerie get so upset about it?

Tina, however, was oblivious to the tension in the air. She got to her feet. "Well, okay, but let's try to get together again before I leave. I might not be back for awhile."

"Sure," Sam said, following them to the door. He bent to give Valerie a kiss, but she turned her head and his lips brushed her cheek. "See you later?" he whispered.

She didn't answer.

The next day was Thursday, and Blackie's was already taking on the appearance of a haunted mansion. Workmen were stringing black and orange ribbon everywhere. Huge fake pumpkins sat in each corner of the casino. Witches on brooms leered from doorways and windows. Skeletons hung from the ceiling on invisible wires.

Sam spotted Valerie in the coffee shop. She was sitting with Ron the security guard. "Hi," Sam said as he approached. "The place looks great, doesn't it?"

"Hi, Sam," Valerie said cooly. "You know Ron."

"Yeah. Hi, Ron."

Sam sat down and ordered coffee. "So ... did you finish your costume?" he asked Valerie, watching her closely.

"Almost," she answered. "I've got a little more to do tonight."

"What are you wearing?"

"It's a surprise. You'll see it tomorrow."

"Well, all right."

"Have you thought about what you're going to wear?" Valerie asked him.

"Yeah," Sam nodded. "I'm going as a cowboy."

"A cowboy! Can't you be a little more creative than that?"

Sam's face dropped. "Well, what's wrong with being a cowboy?"

Valerie turned to Ron. "What are you going to wear, Ron?"

Ron shrugged. "I don't know. I can't think of anything."

Valerie smiled suddenly. "I've got it! Ron, you be a dealer, and Sam, you be a security guard!"

Ron and Sam frowned at each other.

"All you have to do is switch uniforms. You're both about the same size. It's perfect."

"Well, it's okay by me, I guess," Ron said finally.

"Me, too," Sam said. "But if I'm going to be a security guard, I'm wearing a gun."

"We don't wear guns, Sam. I told you that. You'll stick out like a sore thumb."

"Look, it's a costume. I know something about costumes, and a security guard costume needs a gun."

"All right, all right," Valerie said, rolling her eyes. "I'll get you a water pistol from the toy store on my way home tonight."

"Make sure it's black. I don't want a green one. Or a red one."

After work, Sam took his time walking back to the motorhome. Valerie was still acting strange and besides, she was busy tonight. Tina was busy rehearsing. The guys on his crap crew were busy doing something else.

Well, it wouldn't hurt to hit the sack early. Tomorrow was going to be a busy day. Ron would be at Sam's place around nine so they could exchange uniforms. Valerie was coming at nine-thirty with Sam's pistol. That was great, because he'd get a chance to see her costume before anyone else did. And maybe she'd be in a better mood. He certainly couldn't stay mad at her. Hell, he was already thinking about her again.

He was fitting his key in the door when headlights splashed across him and a battered yellow Cadillac convertible shuddered to a stop five feet away. Sam squinted at it in the harsh light. The car was pocked with rust. Dents covered the body from front to back. The exhaust pipe was almost touching the ground. The idling engine sounded like an old cement mixer. What really caught Sam's attention, though, was the front of the car. An enormous set of steer horns was mounted over the radiator. The whole contraption looked like something out of a Buster Keaton movie.

The headlights—one on high, one on low—suddenly blinked off and the car doors creaked open. "Who's there?" Sam called out anxiously.

"Sam? It's me. Tina."

"Oh, hi, Tina. Come on in."

He turned on the lights just as Tina came through the doorway. "I want you to see someone," she announced mysteriously. In through the door walked Buck Beaumont.

"Buck?" Sam said hollowly.

"Yeah. Who are you?"

"Sam Durango."

Buck flashed Tina a dirty look. "Why, you little fart. You told me we were picking up sheet music."

"You guys used to be friends," Tina pouted. "I was just trying to get you back together again."

Sam took a deep breath and stuck out his hand. "Buck, it's good to see you again."

"Yeah," Buck said, taking Sam's hand. "You bet."

"You look great," Sam said, biting his tongue. Buck's face was crisscrossed with worry lines and his eyes were almost lifeless. A black moustache practically hid everything from his nose down. Sam couldn't tell about his hair because Buck was wearing a large white Stetson, but his sideburns were as black and bushy as the moustache, and just as out of place.

"Thanks for the compliment," Buck was saying. "But what the hell happened to you?"

"Well, I cut my hair and let it go gray, and I'm wearing glasses, and I grew a moustache. I may not look the same, but I feel a helluva lot better."

"Glad to hear it," Buck said unconvincingly. "Last I heard, you weren't doing so good."

"Yeah. Well, that's all behind me, Buck. I've got a good job now, and a good woman, and a good life."

Tina stepped between them. "Sam, why don't you come to

Buck's show tonight? I'll even introduce you from the audience."

"I don't know, Tina."

"Oh, come on, Sam," Buck grinned. "It'll be like old times, only I'll be the star this time."

"Okay, Buck," Sam sighed. If it would make Buck feel better to show off in front of him, fine. Then maybe that part of his life would be over for good. "Just give me a minute to change clothes."

"What are you doing with yourself now, anyway?" Buck asked.

"I deal crap at Blackie's." Sam turned and headed for the bathroom.

"Sam?" Tina called. "Where's your telephone? I want to see if Valerie will come with us."

"You're wasting your time. She's working on her costume."

"I want to call her, Sam."

"Tina, I don't have a phone. You're in a motorhome, for crying out loud."

"Then I'll call her from Blackie's," Tina said. "Be back in a minute."

Sam opened an overhead cabinet, pushing aside a stack of twenty dollar bills. He retrieved a pair of jeans and a clean shirt. "Make yourself at home, Buck," he called. "I'll be right back."

"Yeah, okay."

Sam closed the bathroom door and stripped off his work clothes. Then he turned on the water and began washing his face.

"Hey, Sam!" Buck hollered from the other side of the door. "You got any cigarettes in this thing?"

"I don't know, Buck!" Sam hollered back. "Valerie might have left some. Look around."

It was another five minutes before Sam was happy with his appearance. He'd shaved, combed his hair, cleaned his fingernails, rolled on some deodorant, splashed himself with aftershave, and put on his fresh clothes.

He opened the bathroom door. Buck glanced up from the passenger seat of the motorhome, a dazed look in his eyes. "Whoop dee doo dee doo doo," he said to Sam. "Want some?" He held out a half-smoked cigarette. It appeared to be hand-rolled.

"Where'd you get that, Buck?" Sam cried.

"Glove compoopable."

Shit, shit, and double shit.

At that moment, Tina came bounding up the steps. "You were right, Sam. Valerie doesn't want to go. But I thought it was worth—" She stopped suddenly. "What happened to Buck? What did you *do* to him, Sam?"

"I didn't do *anything* to him. He was snooping in the glove compartment and found that—that cigarette you gave me."

"That was two *months* ago! Why didn't you just mount the damn thing on the wall!"

"I totally forgot about it! Honest!"

Tina pushed past Sam and knelt at Buck's feet. "Buck, how do you feel?"

"I feel funny," Buck laughed.

Tina turned to Sam. "Get me a washcloth and some cold water."

Sam hurried to the bathroom and came back with a wet towel. She began to dab at Buck's face as he slowly fell off the seat sideways. His white Stetson rolled across the floor, and now Sam knew why Buck never took his hat off. The poor guy was bald!

"How about some ice cubes?" Sam asked anxiously.

"What are we going to do with ice cubes, Sam? Stick them down his underwear?"

"I'm just trying to be helpful."

"You've done enough already," Tina mumbled, looking at her watch. "Oh my God, look at the time! He's supposed to do his show in less than half an hour."

"Hell, he'll never make it."

"Sam, you're going to have to take his place."

"Oh no you don't. No way!"

"You've got to. There's nobody else who can do it."

Sam groaned. "Damn it, Tina. Why did you have to bring him over here, anyway? I've never seen his show. Does he sing? Does he dance? Does he do rope tricks? I'm going to ruin his career, and mine, too!"

"Did you keep any of your cowboy clothes?"

"Well, yeah, but I made a promise to myself that I'd never—"

"Go put 'em on," Tina ordered.

Sam knew he'd never win this argument. He dashed back to the overhead cabinet, shoved the money aside, and pulled out his tan cowboy suit with curly brown embroidery. With it came his brown and orange shirt with little silver corner-pieces on the collar tips. He'd saved these things for a special occasion, and unfortunately this was it.

When he came back, Tina eyed him critically. "Well, those clothes are a little big for you, but they'll do."

Sam almost said, "That's funny, coming from someone who changes boobs at will." But Tina cut off the thought.

"Have you got any black shoe polish?"

"Yeah, I think so." Damn it, he felt like he was on a scavenger hunt.

"Go get it."

Sam returned with a can of Shinola. Tina popped the lid. "Come here."

He sat at the dining table, resisting the urge to rest his boots on Buck's prone figure. She dabbed at his moustache with the polish. "There," she said. "Now put on Buck's hat and let's see what you look like."

Sam picked up the Stetson and put it on. The hat slid down to his eyebrows. "It's a little big," he said, trying to see Tina from underneath it. "Maybe if we washed it in hot water, it would shrink a couple of sizes."

"We don't have time. Come on, help me get Buck in the car. We've got to get going."

"What about the show? What am I supposed to do?"

"Just tell a few jokes. Then bring out Blue Jay. The crowd loves that. Then introduce me, and I'll finish up with a big song. That's all there is to it, Sam."

"Blue Jay! That damn dog hates me."

Tina exhaled slowly as she and Sam pulled Buck to his feet. "Blue Jay went to doggie heaven years ago. This one's just a toy. He can't hurt you, Sam."

"Blue Jay died?" He let go of Buck's arm and Buck sagged against Tina. "I —I didn't know."

"You just said he hated you."

"Yeah, but I liked *him*."

They got Buck into the back seat of the convertible, then Tina was behind the steering wheel. She squealed out of the parking lot, Sam seated next to her and mumbling to himself.

"What did you say?" she hollered. "I can't hear you!"

"I didn't say anything. I'm rehearsing my lines."

The marquee at Whitey's loomed closer and closer, like a storm beacon on a stormy night.

IN PERSON
BUCK BEAUMONT
And His Wonder Dog Blue Jay
Tickets $2

The car skidded to a stop at the stage door of Whitey's. Tina and Sam helped Buck out of the back seat and walked him inside. A dressing room behind the curtains had Buck's name on the door. Tina pushed it open with her foot, and they sat Buck down at the dressing-room table.

"Buck? Look at me," Tina said, her face inches from his.

"Huh?" His eyes found her for a moment, then glazed over again.

"Don't move. You stay right here. Sam's going to do your show, then you're going to bed."

Buck let out a soft cackle.

Sam walked away, shaking his head. "Damn it, Tina. I can't do this. I'm getting the jitters, for God's sake."

"You'll be fine, Sam. Relax."

"I need a script. I can't work without a script. Or cue cards! How about cue cards? Or maybe a Teleprompter ..."

Suddenly a voice boomed from a loudspeaker. "And now, ladies and gentlemen, Whitey's Casino in Las Vegas, Nevada, proudly presents—"

A drum roll almost scared Sam out of his boots.

"—Buck Beaumont and his wonder dog Blue Jay!"

Velvet curtains opened and there was a smattering of applause from the small audience scattered around the showroom.

"Please, Tina," Sam pleaded, pushing Buck's hat back so

he could see her face. "Don't ask me to do this. I'll do anything else. I'll pay Buck's bills. I'll cook his meals. I'll drive him back to California in his horn-mobile. But *please* don't ask me to do this."

"You're an actor, Sam. So get out there and *act!*"

With that, she gave him a shove and he flailed out across the stage, right into the glare of a spotlight. The applause ended and it was just Sam and the microphone, up against the whole civilized world.

"Howdy, folks," he said, pushing his hat back again. "Welcome to Lost Wages." A couple of titters. Damn, and that was his best line. "I'm Buck Beaumont." Some applause. "I was on TV back around the time of Sam Durango and 'The Vegas Kid.'" Nothing on that one. Damn. "But you may remember me as an actor who has been in the movies." A little applause. "As an actor who has been on television." One person clapped. "As an actor who has been on the stage." Nothing. "In fact, I'm one of the biggest has-beens around." Some snickers. "But I know you're not here to see me. You're here to see my wonder dog Blue Jay." Thunderous applause.

Sam turned and looked offstage. Tina was kneeling next to a small dog and she seemed to be winding it up with a key. Suddenly the dog clip-clopped onto the stage, moving jerkily toward Sam. As it approached, its tail began to wag back and forth, almost like the pendulum on a clock. Back. Forth. Back. Forth.

"Hey, Blue Jay," Sam smiled, once the applause died down. "How're you doing, little buddy?"

The dog bumped into the microphone stand and fell over. The audience groaned.

Sam looked at Tina. She shrugged. Sam tried to stand the dog back up with his boot. Now the dog was on its back.

"Hey, what are you doing?" somebody hollered.

"Leave that dog alone!"

"You big bully!"

Sam got down on his knees and righted Blue Jay, who immediately began to clip-clop toward the edge of the stage. Sam picked him up just before the dog took a swan-dive into the audience. He walked back to the microphone, Blue Jay in his arms. "And now, folks, how about a big hand of applause for our special guest, Miss Tina Forlorne!"

The lights dimmed and Sam felt his way offstage. "You were great, Sam," Tina said, flashing him a smile. She was surrounded by musicians, dancers, singers, acrobats, stilt-walkers, trapeze artists, clowns, and somebody wearing a lion's head. "Go check on Buck," she called as she started onstage. "I'll meet you in the dressing room."

"Okay, Tina," Sam replied. "And break an arm!"

Sam pushed open the dressing room door. "Buck? It's me! You feeling any better?"

No answer. Sam walked inside and looked around. Buck wasn't at the dressing-room table, he wasn't on the couch, he wasn't on the floor. Buck was gone.

Sam stood there with his hands on his hips. What was he supposed to do now? He couldn't leave. Tina wouldn't know what happened to him or Buck. He couldn't stay. In Buck's condition, there was no telling what kind of trouble he would get into. Well, he'd just have to wait until Tina's song was over, then they could search for Buck together. There were only two places he could be, so that narrowed it down a little. He was either in Whitey's Casino, or he was in the car. Yeah, that narrowed it down a little. Hell, Buck could be anywhere.

Suddenly, Sam heard a roar from the audience and Tina came rushing into the room. "You guys ready to go?" she asked. Then her eyes went wide. "Where's Buck? What did you *do* to him, Sam?"

"I didn't do anything to him. He was gone when I got here."

"Shit! I feel like a damn babysitter!"

"Well, I'm thinking he's either in the casino or he's gone off in the car somewhere. So why don't you check to see if the car's still there and I'll look in the casino."

"He didn't go anywhere in the car, Sam. I've got the keys."

"Well, okay then. He's in the casino. Come on, follow me."

Sam and Tina elbowed their way through the crowded gambling hall. Buck wasn't at the bar, in the lounge, in the men's room, in the coffee shop. There was only one place left to look.

"He might be gambling. Tina, check out the slot machines. I'll meet you at the blackjack tables."

Sam went from one blackjack table to the next, but there was no sign of Buck. He stopped at the last table. The dealer was standing with his arms folded. Only one man was at the table, baldheaded, staring grimly into space. Baldheaded?

"Buck?"

"Sam?"

"Buck!"

"Sam!"

"TINA!"

"BUCK!" Tina cried, rushing to his side. "Are you all right?"

"No," Buck groaned. "Let's get out of here."

Sam and Tina followed Buck from the blackjack table. Buck made it as far as the keno lounge, where he sagged into a chair. Tina sat on one side, Sam on the other.

"What happened, Buck?" Tina asked him in a small voice.

"I got to playing blackjack," Buck started slowly. "Couldn't win a hand. I took a marker to try to win back what I lost, then I lost that. I took another marker to try to win back my first marker, then I lost that. Took another marker to—"

"What's the bottom line, Buck?" Sam interrupted. "How much did you lose?"

Buck looked down at the floor, a haunted vacant look in his eyes. "Everything."

"What do you mean, everything?" Tina asked carefully.

"The whole week's pay," Buck said. "Twenty-five thousand dollars."

"You mean, you lost my money, too?" Tina said.

"Everything."

"Shit," Tina said.

"I ain't broke," Buck said proudly. "I got the car." He turned to Sam. "I paid thirty-thousand for it, and I spent another twenty-thousand fixing it up. Tell you what, Sam. Give me twenty-five thousand and it's yours."

"Damn it, Buck, I bought you that car years ago. And it isn't worth spit."

"Hmph," Buck said.

"But why did you play blackjack, Buck?" Tina asked. "You don't know anything about blackjack."

"Yeah," Sam said. "Poker's your game. It always has been."

"Because they didn't have any poker tables," Buck explained, as if he were talking to two six-year-olds.

"What are we going to do, Sam?" Tina asked.

"Let me think." He rubbed his moustache thoughtfully. His hand came away with black shoe polish on it. Suddenly, he grinned. "I've got it! Buck, you stay right here. Don't move this time. Tina, you follow me."

Tina ran to catch up as Sam hurried toward the dice table. "How much money have you got in your purse?" he called over his shoulder.

"I don't know. Thirty dollars max. I was counting on this show, Sam."

"Give it here." Sam opened his wallet and counted his money. "I've got ninety. That gives us a hundred and twenty." He smiled at Tina. "We're in business, kid."

"What are you going to do, Sam?"

"I'm not going to do anything. You're going to do it."

"Do what?"

"Remember how you used to shoot those dice at the beach house? You could make 'em sing."

"So?"

"So you're going to do it again. I'll make the bets, and I'll tell you what to roll. And all you have to do is roll it. Think you can do that?"

Tina grinned. "No problemo. Those dice are putty in my hands."

"Next shooter!" the stickman announced, and the dice were in front of Tina.

Sam tossed a handful of bills to the stickman. "Give me a hundred dollars on twelve!" He whispered to Tina. "Roll a twelve."

Tina picked up the dice and shook them. "COME ON, BOXCARS!" she cried, and the dice went tumbling down the table.

"Twelve craps," the stickman said in a bored voice. A stack of purple chips was pushed in front of Sam.

"Give me a hundred dollars on aces!" he hollered. "Aces this time, Tina," he whispered.

"Aces?" she asked blankly.

"You know—onesies."

"COME ON, ONESIES!" she cried, and the dice bounced down the table.

"Two craps," the stickman said. Another stack of purple chips was placed in front of Sam.

"This is fun," Tina cried as a crowd began to form. "What do you want me to roll now, Sam?"

Sam was counting. He was still nineteen thousand short. "What can I bet on that will pay me back nineteen thousand five hundred and two dollars?" he asked the pit boss.

Without a moment's hesitation, the pit boss replied, "A four hundred and fifty dollar horn high twelve with a two hundred dollar side bet on any craps."

"I'll take it," Sam said. Then to Tina he said, "Roll anything."

Tina picked up the dice. "COME ON, ANYTHING!"

"Twelve craps," the stickman said, and here came seven stacks of purple chips, along with an assortment of greens, browns, and blues. Sam tossed two purple chips to the stickman. "For the boys," he said. Then he gave three purple chips to Tina. "And here's three hundred for you."

"Thanks, Sam!"

Sam put the two one-dollar chips in his pocket and dumped

the rest into Buck's cowboy hat. "Okay, follow me."

"What were the two dollars for?" Tina asked, hurrying to catch up with Sam as he strode across the casino.

"To pay Valerie back for my water pistol."

Tina stopped, scratched her head, then raced to catch up with Sam again.

Buck was still slumped in the chair where Sam and Tina had left him.

"Sam got the money back," Tina grinned.

"Thanks to Tina," Sam added.

"I really appreciate this," Buck smiled, reaching for the cowboy hat.

"Not so fast," Sam said. "If you want this money back, you're going to have to work for it."

"What do you mean?"

Sam sat down next to Buck. "There's a five hundred thousand dollar poker tournament at Blackie's tomorrow."

Buck whistled.

"There's also a twenty-five thousand dollar entry fee. Now here's my proposition. You're going to play in that tournament. If you win, you get the twenty-five thousand back, and I get the rest."

"And if I lose?"

"Then we're right back where we started."

Buck scowled. "No deal. If I win, I want half the money. I'm the one doing the work."

"The money's not for me, Buck. I'm going to use it to buy Blackie's. And if I do buy the joint, I'll promise you this. Anytime you want to perform in Vegas with Blue Jay, the showroom's yours."

Buck was silent, his gaze going from Sam to his cowboy hat.

"Do it, Buck!" Tina cried. "What have you got to lose?"

"Okay," Buck said finally. "I'll do it. But I'm not doing it for you, Sam. I'm not doing it for you either, Tina. I'm not even doing it just to play in the showroom. I'm doing it because it's a challenge, and I've always faced a challenge head on. I'm doing it for all the little people out there who never had a chance in life. I'm doing it—"

"For the twenty-five thousand dollars to pay off your markers," Sam finished.

Buck slowly nodded his head.

"What time does the tournament start?" Tina asked anxiously.

"Noon," Sam said. "So why don't you two get some sleep, then meet me at my place around eight? That'll give us plenty of time to go over everything."

"Eight?" Tina cried. "Sam, it's a quarter to eight now!"

"In the *morning*?" Shit, shit, and double shit. "Well, come on then, Buck. Let's go. And Tina?"

"I know," Tina said wearily. "Follow you."

Sam converted the chips into currency, then the three of them drove back to the motorhome. Sam couldn't believe it was morning already, and even the Nevada sun, pale behind a thin layer of clouds, stung his eyes. He hadn't stayed up all night since his high school graduation party. Still, he wasn't really that tired, even though he knew it was the adrenaline pumping through his system that energized him.

"Get some coffee going," he told Tina as they filed inside. "We're going to need lots of coffee."

"You got any cigarettes in this thing?" Buck asked.

"Shut up, Buck!" Tina said.

Sam set Buck's cowboy hat on top of the driver's seat, then went to the refrigerator for sausage and eggs. A stack of ten dollar bills fell to the floor. Sam quickly stuffed the money back inside, then crossed to the stove. "How do you like your eggs, Buck?" he asked, turning on the fire.

"Yeah, I like 'em okay."

Sam shook his head—same old Buck—then cracked an egg open. Looking at the busted yolk, he said, "Well, you're getting them scrambled."

They'd just finished breakfast when there was a knock on the door. Sam peeped through the window. "It's Ron. We're changing uniforms for the masquerade party today," he explained.

"Hi," Ron said, climbing the steps.

"Morning," Sam answered. "Ron, I want you to meet some friends of mine. This is Buck, and this is Tina."

As the others talked, Sam went to the closet and got out a pair of black slacks, a black shirt, a black apron, and a white tie, handing them all to Ron. In return, Ron handed Sam a neatly folded security uniform, a flashlight, and a pair of handcuffs.

"Want some breakfast?" Sam asked.

"No, I've just got time to change. I'm working the early shift."

Ron disappeared into the bathroom with Sam's clothes, while Tina fiddled with the television. "How do you turn this thing on, Sam?"

"Uh, pair of pliers, on top of the refrigerator," Sam replied absently, pouring Buck another cup of coffee.

"In other news, a weeks-long nationwide dragnet has turned up no sign of escaped convicts Stitch Mason and Louie 'The Blade' Salvatore. Authorities believe the two may be trying to flee the country in a light-blue Ford Fairlane. A reward of ten thousand dollars has been offered to anyone with information on the whereabouts of these dangerous criminals, including a two hundred and fifty dollar reward from the Ace Novelty Company."

"Tina, turn that thing down!" Sam hollered. "We're trying to think."

Ron opened the bathroom door. "Well, how do I look?" he asked, looking at Sam skeptically.

"You look like a dealer," Sam announced. "Let me try on your stuff."

Sam closed the bathroom door and began to change out of his cowboy clothes. He splashed cold water on his face, washed the shoe polish out of his moustache, brushed his teeth, slapped on some aftershave, and ran a comb through his hair. After putting on Ron's security uniform, he strapped on his dusty old holster, then studied himself in the mirror. With any luck, this would be the last time he'd ever have to wear a costume.

"What do you think, Ron?" he asked, coming out of the bathroom in his stocking feet.

"Ron's gone," Buck answered absently. "He said he'd see you at work."

"Oh. Well, what do you think, Tina?"

"Tina's gone. She said she had to get some sleep."

"Oh. Well, what do you think, Buck?"

"You look like Smokey the Bear," Buck said. "Come on, let's play a few hands of poker. I need the practice."

Just as Sam sat down at the table, someone knocked on the door. "It's Valerie!" Sam said, looking through the window and unable to control his excitement. "She's my girlfriend."

"Hi, Sam," Valerie smiled as she came inside. Then she saw Buck at the dining table and her face went white. "Buck?" she asked hollowly.

"Yeah, hi," Buck answered, not looking up as he shuffled a deck of cards.

"You two know each other?" Sam asked.

"No," Valerie said hurriedly. "I—I just recognize him is all."

Buck dealt himself a hand of solitaire. "We better get going pretty soon," he said, giving Sam a weary glance.

"Where's your costume?" Sam asked Valerie.

"It's in the car. I'm going to put it on now."

"Did you—did you get my gun?"

"It's in the car, Sam."

"Great!"

Valerie looked at him closely. "Sam, you look terrible."

"I feel fine."

"Your eyes are bright red. Have you been drinking?"

"No, I didn't get any sleep last night. That's all."

"Why not?"

He lowered his voice so Buck couldn't hear him. "Because Buck smoked one of Tina's cigarettes, so I had to do his show at Whitey's, then he lost all his money playing blackjack, so Tina and I shot crap and I won it all back, and now we're using the money to enter Buck in the poker tournament at Blackie's, and if he wins he gets his money back, and I'm going to take the rest of it and buy Blackie's from Vinnie the Moochie!"

"What?"

"I said—"

"I know what you said, Sam. But what's all this about the poker tournament? You can't play in the poker tournament."

"*I'm* not playing in the tournament. *Buck* is. I'm just backing him, that's all."

Valerie sighed. "It's the same thing, Sam. If you're backing him, then you're in the tournament, too."

"Well, okay, then I'm in the tournament, too. So what?"

"Employees can't gamble where they work. If somebody finds out, Blackie's could lose its gambling license and the whole place could close."

"Who's going to find out, Valerie? The only ones who know about it are you, me, Tina, Buck, and maybe Ron."

"Ron?"

"Yeah, he was over here a few minutes ago to change clothes. And damn it, I introduced him to Buck!"

"Well, there you go. If Ron knows about it, he's going to tell the rest of the security people and the next thing you know it'll be all over the casino!"

Damn. "What are we going to do?"

"Do you really want to go through with this, Sam?"

"Yeah. How else will I ever be able to buy Blackie's?"

Valerie sighed again. "All right, then. He'll just have to wear a costume like the rest of us. After all, it *is* Halloween."

"Buck, you've got to wear a costume!" Sam hollered.

"Whatever," Buck mumbled from the table, half-asleep.

"And I know just what to get him," Valerie smiled. "Hold the fort. I'll be right back."

Valerie hurried out the door. Sam walked over to the dining table and sat down. "Okay, let's practice for a few minutes," he said. "And Buck, drink some more coffee. You're going to need it."

Another hour passed before Valerie returned. She was carrying two boxes, a wig, a small suitcase, and a makeup kit. Sam and Buck looked over her shoulder as she opened the boxes.

"What the hell is this?" Buck demanded. "It looks like a damn dress!"

"It is a dress," Valerie smiled.

"And these look like high-heel shoes."

"They are high-heel shoes."

"And what's this? Panty hose! No! Damn it now, if you think I'm going to play poker dressed up like some floozie, then you got another thing coming!"

"You owe Whitey's twenty-five thousand, Buck," Sam reminded him. "Take it or leave it."

"You can change in the bathroom," Valerie prompted.

Buck swept the clothing off the table and stomped toward the bathroom.

"Not yet, Buck," Valerie said. "I need to go in there for a minute."

"Yeah," Sam grinned. "Remember, Buck—ladies first."

Valerie picked up the small suitcase and disappeared into the bathroom. The door opened moments later. "Okay, Buck. It's all yours."

Buck slammed the door.

"Where'd you get those clothes?" Sam grinned as he poured himself another cup of coffee. "Are they having a fire sale at Omar the Tentmaker's?"

"No, I got them at Bertha's Ample Duds over on Charleston. It was the last thirty-two petite in the store."

Sam guffawed. "You know what, Valerie? I'm to the point now where I don't even care if Buck wins or not. It's going to be worth twenty-five thousand just to see him wearing lipstick."

"Twenty-five thousand ... Sam, that's a lot of money. It sounds so scary."

"Oh, it'll be okay." Then Sam frowned. "There is one thing,

though. What's to keep Buck from just taking off with the money if he wins tonight?"

"Well, I don't think he will."

"Oh?"

"Do you know what I was doing in the bathroom?"

"That's okay, Valerie. You don't have to—"

"I was setting up an eight-millimeter camera. It's hidden behind your shower curtain. Buck's putting on panty hose and a brassiere and a size thirty-two dress, and I'm getting it all on film!"

"Whoa! Is that what you call blackmail?"

"Well, let's just call it insurance."

The bathroom door slowly opened. Buck clomped down the hall in his high- heel shoes. The aqua-colored dress he wore was accented by a thin orange belt and bright yellow pantyhose. "What do you think?" he asked quietly. "I stuffed some toilet paper in the top, but I might have overdone it."

"No, you look fine," Valerie said as she studied him. "But the moustache and sideburns have got to go."

"Can't we just cover 'em up with powder or something? I got two years invested in that moustache."

"It'll grow back," Sam said. "The important thing is that nobody in the casino knows who you are. Valerie's right, Buck. You've got to get rid of the stash and burns."

Buck clomped back into the bathroom.

"You know, he doesn't really look that bad, Sam. Purple is Buck's color."

"I'll say," Sam grinned. "Hell, I'm getting a boner."

Buck clomped out of the bathroom again. His face was clean-shaven. "I feel naked," he said.

"Come sit at the table," Valerie said. "I want to do your face."

Sam stood behind her as she opened her makeup kit. "Foundation," she said to Sam. He rummaged through the kit. "Foundation," he said, passing her a small jar.

"Blush," she said.

"Blush."

"Lipstick."

"Lip liner."

"Mascara."

"Eyebrow shadow."

"Scalpel."

"Scalpel?" Buck screamed.

"Relax, Buck. I'm just cutting the price tag off your dress."

Sam studied Buck's face as Valerie placed a blonde wig on top of Buck's bald head. "What do you think, Sam?"

"He looks good. Except for his eyebrows. They're too bushy."

"I ain't cutting my eyebrows off," Buck said defiantly. "It's my last vestige of manhood, for God's sake."

Valerie hunted through her purse, and came out holding a pair of glasses with tiny rose-colored lenses. They were the ones Sam wore at the beach. "Try these on, Buck."

Buck put on the glasses and clomped to the bathroom mirror.

"Wait," Valerie said, running after him. "You forgot your gloves."

"What time is it getting to be?" Sam yawned. "I've got to be at work at ten."

"Good grief, Sam, why didn't you say something sooner? It's eleven- fifteen!"

Sam grabbed the cowboy hat full of money and shoved it at Buck. He kissed Valerie's cheek as he ran past. "I'll see you at work!" he hollered. "And good luck, Buck." He was halfway across the parking lot when he remembered his gun. Racing back to Valerie's car, he snatched the water pistol out of a shopping bag and stuck it in his holster.

Damn! He'd never been late to work in his entire life, not even when he worked at the studio and had to be at make-up at five in the morning. Well, he would have to do the right thing and tell the truth, that's all. And—and just what was the truth? That he'd been up all night shooting crap so he could win enough money to buy a casino by sponsoring a man who was dressed like a woman who was in a dad-blasted poker tournament? No, this was one of those little moments in life when a man had to do the wrong thing in order to do the right thing. He had to lie.

"Sorry I'm late," Sam panted as he got to the dice table. "I overslept."

"Go see Shorty," the pit boss said. Sam looked around, and saw a man five feet tall behind the podium. "Are you Shorty?"

"I'm Shorty."

"I'm late for work. I overslept."

"Go see Tiny."

Sam saw a man four feet tall at the next podium. "Are you Tiny?"

"I'm Tiny."

"I'm late. I overslept."

"Go see Pee Wee."

Suddenly Sam was in shadows, staring up at a man almost seven feet tall.

"Are you Pee Wee?"

"I'M PEE WEE."

"I'm late. I overslept."

"DON'T DO IT AGAIN."

The poker tournament got under way at five minutes after twelve. Buck clomped up to the registration desk just before the noon deadline. The cashier counted out his entry fee, then Buck followed her past the display of the half-million dollars to an empty spot at one of the poker tables. His name tag read "Becky Sunnybrook," which was another of Valerie's hare-brained ideas. He couldn't wait to get back to Hollywood, where life was a hell of a lot simpler. Right now, though, he had to concentrate on playing poker and winning back the money he lost so he could buy back his markers at Whitey's.

There were thirty-six entrants in the tournament, with six players at each table. The game was five-card stud, one of Buck's favorites. Each player started out with twenty-five thousand dollars in chips. The ante for the first round was ten dollars a hand. At the end of one hour, the three players at each table with the most money would advance to the second round.

The ante for the second round was one hundred dollars a hand. At the end of the second hour, the field would be trimmed to the twelve players with the most money left. After another hour, at an ante of five hundred dollars per hand, the field would be cut to six. Then these six players would meet in the finals, where the ante would be raised to one thousand dollars a hand. They would continue to play until one man had all the chips. Or in this case, Buck thought as he pushed up his bosom, one woman.

He eyed the other players at his table as the first round got under way. Seated on Buck's right was a short Mexican man wearing thick glasses. The man smiled at Buck. Buck smiled back. He might as well be sociable.

A cocktail waitress stopped at Buck's side. She looked exactly like Dorothy in the movie *Wizard of* Oz. Pigtails, gingham dress, red ruby shoes. "Would you like some coffee, Becky?" she asked him sweetly.

"No, thanks," Buck said in a falsetto voice. "Bring me a Jack Daniels."

"I think you'd better have coffee, Becky," Dorothy said in a firmer voice.

"Jack Daniels, please," Buck falsettoed. "Double shot, straight up."

"You're getting coffee, Buck," Dorothy hissed in his ear.

Oh God, it was Valerie, dressed in her damn Halloween costume.

The hour droned by and Buck got one bad hand after another. Then his luck changed. Here came four cards to a full house, and he drew a third jack to fill his boat. That won him enough to advance to the second round. One of the other two winners was the Mexican man with the thick glasses.

Buck was getting his confidence back. Sure, he was playing against some of the top poker players in the country, and he had to watch how he talked and how he acted. But it was just poker. He wasn't assembling a nuclear warhead or even changing washers in a leaky faucet. He was only playing cards! And he was good at it. The Mexican man with the thick glasses smiled at Buck, as though he were reading Buck's mind. Buck smiled back.

"More coffee, Becky?" Valerie asked him.

"Yeah," Buck grumbled. Then, in his falsetto voice, "Yes, please."

Another hour ticked by. A crowd had gathered by now, but Buck didn't see the people. He didn't hear the noise. All he saw were the cards in his hand, and the chips on the table. "Raise you two hundred," a man in a Hawaiian shirt said.

"Fold," said a second man.

"I'm out," said another.

"I'll see that two hundred," Buck said slowly in his falsetto voice. "And I'll bump you another three hundred."

The Mexican man shook his head and threw his cards in.

"I'll see you," Hawaiian Shirt said, tossing three one-hundred-dollar chips into the pot. "What have you got?"

Buck turned over a five, nine, queen, jack, ace. They were all spades. "Flush," he trilled.

"Damn!" Hawaiian Shirt cried. "You're the luckiest woman I've ever seen."

"Thank you, big boy," Buck smiled coyly.

They were down to two tables now, and Buck and the Mexican man were still in the thick of it.

• • •

A black Ford Fairlane turned into the parking lot at Blackie's and came to a stop near a motorhome with a red stripe down the side.

Stitch Mason turned and gave his passenger a sneer. "Now what?" he asked Lou.

"Now we make a little withdrawal. Come on, let's go."

Stitch and Louie started toward the entrance. The marquee in front read:

MASQUERADE PARTY FRIDAY
WEAR A COSTUME AND GET FREE DRINKS
$500,000 POKER TOURNAMENT

"Look, Lou," Stitch exclaimed. "Everybody's wearing costumes."

Louie looked at Stitch's wrinkled business suit, then down at the one he was wearing. "This ain't gonna work, Stitch. We'll never get out the door dressed like this."

"Waddaya got in mind, Lou?"

"Let's go inside. I'll think of something."

Stitch and Louie entered the casino and saw two men walking toward the restrooms. One was wearing a chicken outfit and the other was dressed as an alligator. Louie nodded at Stitch. Stitch nodded back. They followed the chicken and alligator into the men's room.

Two minutes later, the door to the men's room opened again. Out came a chicken and an alligator. "How do I look, Stitch?" the chicken asked.

"You look cheep, cheep, cheep," the alligator answered. They laughed, then headed for the casino, where the poker tournament was being held.

They were just like any other costume-clad visitors to Blackie's, except one of them had a .45 under his right wing.

Sam looked up from the dice table. Judy Garland's double from *Wizard of Oz* was waving at him from across the room. She was gorgeous. Beautiful face, tight little body, short, almost an exact duplicate of Valerie. Then he forgot all about Judy Garland and started thinking about Valerie again, wondering what kind of costume she was wearing today. He'd never gotten a chance to see it yet.

Judy Garland's double waved at him again. Sam smiled and nodded impatiently. "You look nice," he mouthed. Some women will do anything for a compliment.

Judy Garland came a few feet closer. "It's me," she mouthed back.

Valerie? Sam's mouth dropped open. How was this for fate? He sees a beautiful woman from afar, doesn't give her a second thought, gets all dreamy about Valerie, and she turns out to *be* Valerie!

"What time do you get off?" Valerie mouthed.

"What?"

"What—time—do you—get—off?"

"Six—o—clock."

"See—you—in the—poker—room."

"Oh—kay." Then he mouthed, "I—love—you." Too late. She was already gone.

Six players were left in the poker tournament:

A tall bone-thin man in a black suit;

Young red-faced man in blue jeans and a flannel shirt;
Lanky Texan in a buckskin jacket;
Fat perspiring man with a white flower in his lapel;
Mexican man wearing thick glasses,
A six-foot-tall woman in an aqua dress.

A dealer in a Fred Flintstone costume dealt the cards, and each player studied his hand quietly. Cigarette smoke drifted lazily over the table. The crowd pushed closer, but the room was deathly still. The only sound was the tiny clink of glasses as Valerie served each player. Another clink, this one a bit louder. The Texan had dropped a one-hundred-dollar chip on her serving tray. Clink, and another one-hundred-dollar chip, this one from the Mexican man. Clink, and a one-dollar chip from Buck.

Valerie glared at him as she moved away from the table, but Buck stared coldly at his cards. King of clubs. King of hearts. King of diamonds. King of spades. Buck's heart was in his throat. This was the hand he'd waited for all his life, but he would have to play it very carefully. One false move and he'd scare everybody out. "Raise five dollars," he said in his falsetto voice.

"Call."
"Call."
"Call."
"Call."

"See the five dollars and raise twenty-thousand," the fat man said.

Buck studied his cards again. There they were, four cowboys, all in a row. "See the twenty and raise fifty thousand."

An excited murmur from the crowd, and then those dreaded words:

"Call."
"Call."
"Call."
"Call."

"See the fifty thousand and raise twenty-five thousand," the fat man said. Buck counted the chips in front of him; Fifty, fifty-one, fifty-two thousand, two hundred; "See the twenty-five thousand and raise fifty-two thousand, two hundred dollars."

"Call."

"Call."

"Call."

"Call."

"Call," the fat man said.

It was all on the table now. This was it. Five people were going to walk out of this room with shattered dreams and bitter memories. There would only be one winner, one champion, one star in the sky tonight.

The crowd surged closer as the bone-thin man in the black suit turned over his cards. Four nines. The young red-faced man in the flannel shirt turned over his cards. Four tens. The Texan in the buckskin jacket turned over his cards. Four jacks. The perspiring fat man turned over his cards. Four queens.

Buck turned over his cards. King of clubs, king of hearts, king of diamonds, king of spades.

The Mexican man with the thick glasses looked at Buck's cards, then back at his own hand. He smiled at Buck. Buck smiled back. The Mexican man looked at his cards again. Then he threw them on the table, face down. "You ween," he said.

There was a tremendous roar from the crowd, then Vinnie Despuchi was standing in front of Buck. He was dressed as a king, and there was a crown on his head. "Congratulations, ma'am," he said.

"Why, thank yew," Buck replied in his falsetto voice.

Vinnie called to Valerie. "Bring out the champagne, honey! It's time to celebrate!" He strode across the room and put the five hundred thousand dollars into a black attaché case. Everyone's attention was on the money, so no one saw Buck turn over the Mexican man's cards, which were still lying face down on the table. Ace of spades, ace of hearts, ace of diamonds, ace of clubs. He looked at the Mexican man. The man smiled. Buck smiled back.

Vinnie was back, the attaché case in his hand. "And now, on behalf of Blackie's Casino in Las Vegas, Nevada, I present the grand prize of five hundred thousand dollars to the winner of our Halloween poker tournament—Miss Becky Sunnybrook!"

Valerie handed Buck a glass of champagne as the crowd began to applaud.

Suddenly, someone hollered, "Gimme that suitcase!" From behind tiny rose-colored lenses, Buck saw an alligator wrestle the attaché case away from Vinnie. Someone else, dressed in a chicken outfit, was holding Valerie, and he had a gun in his hand.

The room went quiet again. "I want all the security people up here on the double!" the chicken clucked. Four security officers reluctantly stepped forward. Three were Elvis look-alikes; the fourth was dressed as a dealer. "Drop those walkie-talkies, handcuffs, and flashlights," the alligator growled.

• • •

Sam was walking down the hall toward the poker room when he heard the roar of the crowd. The tournament must be over. He quickened his step, then realized it was quiet again. Maybe the tournament wasn't over, and now he'd get to see the grand finale. His whole life hinged on Buck winning today, yet he wasn't even nervous. He was tired, yes, and he could probably fall asleep on a treadmill, but he wasn't nervous. Half-dead would be more like it.

The crowd made way for him as he approached the poker room. "Thank you," he said to a spectator. "Thanks," to another. Then he remembered he was dressed in a security uniform. Well, he might as well go along with the joke. "Step aside," he said to the next person. Then, "All right, buddy, move it!"

Suddenly he was face to face with Vinnie, and Valerie, and Buck, and a chicken, and an alligator. Chicken? Alligator? Sam almost smiled. Vinnie the Poochie was throwing one helluva

Halloween party.

The chicken turned toward Sam. He was holding Valerie, and there was a gun in his hand. "Well, if it ain't the head security man," he sneered. "We've been waiting for you."

"Let her go," Sam said softly, using his Vegas Kid voice and biting his tongue to keep from laughing.

"You hear that, Stitch? The rent-a-cop's giving orders."

"I'm telling you for the last time," Sam said. "Let her go."

"She's going, all right. She's going with us. Right out the front door."

This was probably where he was supposed to go for his gun and foil the whole thing. Then the crowd would holler "Surprise!" and everyone would clap and cheer, and the music would start, and he could go to his motorhome and get some damn sleep. So almost in a dream trance, Sam drew the water pistol from his holster. At the same instant, the chicken aimed his gun at Sam and squeezed the trigger.

The chicken's gun made a little popping noise, and a small stick slid out of the barrel. From the stick, a tiny red flag unfurled. On the flag was the word Bang!

"What the hell?" the chicken grunted.

Sam aimed his water pistol at the alligator. "Now hand over that suitcase," he said, now fully in Vegas Kid mode. God, it was just like old times.

The alligator threw the attaché case at Sam, catching him square in the chest and knocking him to the floor. Stitch and Louie raced for the casino entrance, shoving spectators aside as they fled. The four security guards ran to the pile of handcuffs, flashlights, and walkie-talkies. Then they chased after the two convicts.

"Are you all right, Sam?" Valerie asked tenderly, kneeling beside him.

"Sure, I'm fine," Sam grinned. "What a party, huh?"

"Party?" Valerie exclaimed. "This isn't the party. Buck won the tournament and those two creeps were trying to steal the prize money!"

Sam's eyes rolled back in his head and he fainted dead away.

Stitch and Louie went flying out the front door of the casino. A bread truck was parked a few feet away, the motor idling noisily. "We'll never make it to the car, Stitch," Louie gasped. "Quick! The back of that truck!"

The two hopped in, then slammed the door shut. Moments later, the four security guards dashed past, disappearing into the darkness.

"What now, Lou?" Stitch whispered.

"We go where the truck goes," Louie whispered back. He picked up a package of cinnamon rolls and tore the wrapper open. "You hungry?" he whispered.

"Yeah. But could I have mine heated with some melted butter on top?"

The front door of the truck opened and a deliveryman hauled himself into the cab. He shifted the truck into gear and the bread truck rumbled out onto the Strip.

• • •

Sam opened his eyes. Swimming into focus were the faces of King Vinnie, Judy Garland, a perspiring fat man with a white flower in his lapel, a tall woman in an aqua dress, and a Mexican man wearing thick glasses.

"How do you feel, Sam?" Dorothy asked him.

"Toto?" Sam mumbled.

"It's me! Valerie!"

"My back hurts," Sam groaned. "He must have shot me in the back."

"Actually, Sam, you're lying on your handcuffs."

Valerie helped him to his feet and the crowd began to applaud again.

Buck gave him a weak smile, then edged closer. "Can I talk to you a minute? Alone?"

"Yeah, sure," Sam said, following Buck to the corner.

"I've—I've met someone."

"That's great," Sam said, searching the poker room for some gorgeous dame wearing furs and diamond rings. But the only person near Buck was the Mexican man with the thick glasses, smiling.

"His name is Pancho," Buck said. "He's a movie producer from Mexico. He wants me to fly to Acapulco with him. He says he's going to make me a star."

"Like that?" Sam asked, nodding at Buck's dress.

"Well, I figure as soon as I get to Mexico I'll change into some regular clothes again. It may take a few days to bring him around, but I think I can do it." Buck smiled shyly. "He likes me a lot."

"What about your money? I owe you twenty-five thousand."

"Yeah, which goes to Whitey's to pay off my markers. You can take care of that for me, can't you?"

"Sure, but what about the money Whitey's owes you and Tina?"

"That goes automatically to Larry Noble. He'll pay twelve thousand five hundred to Tina and the other fifty-eight people in her show. That leaves ten thousand. I'll wire you for it when I get settled."

"What about your car? The Smithsonian Institution might want to buy it."

"Tina can use it until I get back. Tell her to be careful shifting from second to third, though. Sometimes it goes into reverse."

"So when do you leave?" Sam asked.

"Ponchie's already called the airport, and they're warming up his Lear jet right now."

"Lear jet? Why, you little golddigger, you."

"One more thing, Sam," Buck said, grabbing Sam's arm. "I've got to borrow some of your clothes. And a suitcase to carry them in. I don't have time to go back to my hotel."

"Sure," Sam said. "Get the money and let's go."

Buck returned with the attaché case, then said something to Pancho in broken Spanish. Pancho smiled and walked away. "He's bringing the limousine around back to the motorhome," Buck explained, picking up the attaché case in his gloved hand.

"Better let me carry that," Sam said, taking the attaché case from Buck. "You might break a heel." He'd never had half a million dollars in his hands before. Damn, money was heavy.

"What's it feel like?" Valerie asked, sidling up to Sam.

"Feels good," Sam huffed. "Here, take it."

A bread truck rolled down the highway. Louie sneaked a look out the window from behind a stack of boxes. They were off the Strip in a section of town unfamiliar to him. A jumbo jet roared out of the sky, and overhead another big plane circled. Hell, this was perfect, Louie grinned from behind his chicken face. They were at the damn airport!

The truck turned down a side road and continued through a gate. The driver slowed down, then the truck stopped. With a squeak, the driver's door opened and the deliveryman got out.

Stitch and Louie hid in the shadows while the deliveryman stacked a load of bread and pastries onto a trundle. He slammed the back door shut, then he was gone.

Louie edged the door open again. They were parked alongside a private runway. He motioned to Stitch and the two hopped out of the truck. Several small planes sat nearby on the runway, but only one looked like it was being prepared for takeoff. Its interior lights were on, the stairwell was down, and a man in a flight jacket was checking the landing gear.

"Hey, Artie!" crackled a voice over the P.A. system. "You're got a phone call."

Stitch and Louie crouched behind an oleander bush, watching as Artie walked toward a maintenance building at the end of the runway.

"Are you thinking what I'm thinking?" Stitch whispered.

"Yeah," Louie whispered.

"Okay, on twelve," Stitch whispered. "One ... two ... three ..."

"Oh, the hell with it," Louie said. "Come on, let's go!"

Sam tried the door of the motorhome. It was locked.

"Here's your key, Sam," Valerie said. "I locked the motor house when I left this morning."

"Thanks." Sam unlocked the door and turned on the lights. Buck clomped inside and waited while Sam sorted through his clothes. "Here you go, Buck. Undies, hankies, socksies ..."

"Oh, knock it off, Sam," Buck grumbled.

"Here's a pair of boots, and my western suit," Sam said, sniffing it. "You might want to get it dry cleaned."

Buck took a sniff. "Why? Smells all right to me. Have you got a little suitcase or something?"

Sam scratched his chin. "No, but I'll tell you what. Let me dump all the money out of this attaché case, so you can use it."

He snapped open the case and turned it over. Stacks of neatly packaged hundred dollar bills spilled out over the dining table.

"Just remember where you got it," Buck said, cramming the clothes inside the attaché case.

"I will, Buck," Sam said. "And remember what I said. Whenever you want to come back to Vegas, the showroom at Blackie's is yours."

A horn tooted outside. "Well, that's probably Ponchie," Buck said. "Guess I'll be going." He stuck out a gloved hand and Sam shook it. Then he turned to Valerie. "Can I ask you something before I go?"

Valerie's face paled. "Sure, Buck."

"Is my lipstick on straight?"

The motorhome door closed and Sam and Valerie were alone at last. They smiled warmly at each other. "What are we going to do with all this money?" she asked him quietly.

Sam picked up two packets and opened an overhead compartment. A shower of green bills rained down. There were one dollar bills, five dollar bills, ten dollar bills, twenty dollar bills.

"Sam! Where did all this money come from?"

"Oh, I've been saving it. I meant to go to the bank, but I just haven't gotten around to it." Sam began stuffing the rest of the packets into the compartment.

"That was nice, Sam," Valerie said, sitting down at the table.

"What was?"

"What you said to Buck. About him always having a place to perform at Blackie's. Nice."

"Well, I've been carrying around a lot of hurt for a long time, and after all these years I find out that Buck's been doing the same thing. I guess we're a lot alike after all."

Valerie stood and stretched. "I don't know about you, but I could use a drink."

"All I've got is bourbon. Is that okay?"

"Do you have any Cokes?"

"In the refrigerator."

She opened the refrigerator and more green bills spilled out. There were one dollar bills, five dollar bills, ten dollar bills, twenty dollar bills.

"I've heard of pennies from heaven," she laughed, "but this is ridiculous." Blam, blam, blam.

"Someone's at the door!" Valerie cried.

Sam quickly closed the overhead compartment and carried the rest of the money into the bathroom. He looked around frantically for a hiding place, then dumped the money into the shower stall. "See who it is!" he hollered.

Valerie eased the door open.

"Trick or treat," two youngsters announced. One was dressed as an escaped convict, the other as a policeman.

"Oh, Sam, I forgot," Valerie smiled. "It's Halloween."

"We're in a damn parking lot, for God's sake! What kind of parents would let their kids go begging for candy in a goddamn parking lot?"

"Sam! Otch-way oar-yay anguage-lay."

"Oh, sorry, kids." Sam rummaged through a kitchen cabinet, then returned to the door. "Here's a can of pork and beans for you, and a frying pan for you."

Valerie closed the door.

Blam, blam, blam.

"Trick or treat."

"Cowboy hat for you, hairbrush for you, pouch of tobacco for you."

Blam, blam, blam.

"An egg for you, deck of cards for you, road map for you."

Blam, blam, blam.

"Uh, do you kids like bourbon?"

A pearl-white limousine coasted to a stop next to the Lear jet. The pilot watched as a chauffeur opened the back door. Out stepped a Mexican man wearing thick glasses. Then an extremely tall woman carrying a black attaché case got out of the car. The Mexican man put an arm around her waist and led her to the plane.

"Ees the plane ready, Ottie?" Pancho asked him.

"Si, Señor Morales," Artie smiled. "Evening, ma'am."

"Hello," Buck said in his falsetto voice.

"Tell him I've got to call flight control and then we can take off," the pilot said to Buck.

Buck turned to Pancho. "Flight control telefono, Ponchie, y muy pronto vamanos."

"Bueno, Becky," Pancho grinned.

The chauffeur carried Pancho's bags onto the plane. Buck looked around the small jet in awe as Pancho helped him inside. There were plush seats, stained-glass portholes, wood-paneled walls, a curved bar, a theater screen on the front wall, a built-in stereo under a dressing table, soft muted lights, and velvet curtains at the back of the passenger cabin. The chauffeur pushed the curtains aside, set the luggage down, then tipped his cap and left.

Artie climbed the steps and pulled up the stairwell. "Tell Señor Morales we should be in Acapulco around eight o'clock."

Pancho turned to Buck with a quizzical look on his face. "Que dicé?"

"Acapulkie a la ocho, Ponchie."

"Marveloso!"

The small jet thundered down the runway, then the lights of Las Vegas were miles below them. Somewhere down there, Sam and that Valerie woman were sifting through half a million dollars in cold cash that by all rights should have been his. Well, actually, it should have been Ponchie's. Buck's eyes closed as he went over the poker tournament again in his mind.

He was holding four kings, and Ponchie folded with four aces. All Ponchie had to do was show his cards. The money would have been his and Buck would have been up the creek without a paddle. But Ponchie, being the true gentleman that he was, had simply smiled and dropped out of the game, letting Buck get all the glory. Buck was still up the creek, but at least he had a paddle now. And the paddle owned a Lear jet and a movie studio.

"Ponchie? Yo quiero uno grande Jack Daniels, por favor."

"Si, mi corazon," Pancho grinned, unbuckling his seat belt and moving to the bar.

The velvet curtains at the back of the plane opened an inch. A chicken face looked out. He saw a Mexican man standing at the bar and a woman in an aqua dress sitting in one of the seats with a black attaché case at her feet. The velvet curtains closed. "Stitch," the chicken whispered. "It's the big broad from the poker tournament. And she's still got the money!"

"Great!" the alligator whispered. "Now if this plane is only going to Mexico, everything would be perfect!"

23

Sam smiled gratefully as Valerie brought coffee to the table. She sat across from him and sipped from her cup quietly.

"What are you thinking about?" she asked him.

"You. Me. Us. And it just dawned on me that I don't know that much about you."

Valerie frowned. "Well, I'm single."

"That's a relief," Sam grinned.

"I grew up in California. My father raised me. I never knew my mother. She died when I was just a baby."

Sam reached across the table and took her hand. "My mother died when I was just a baby," he said. "And my *father* raised *me*."

Her fingers were tracing little loops on his hand. "We're alike in so many ways, Sam. I feel like we've known each other forever."

"Let's make a promise," he said tenderly. "Let's always be honest with each other. I want to share everything with you."

Her hand went limp in his. She was peering out the window, biting her lip.

"What's wrong, sweetheart?"

"Oh, Sam, I haven't been honest with you from the beginning!" Her voice quivered and her eyes welled up. "I guess it's time I told you the truth about everything." Dabbing at her eyes with a handkerchief, she let out a slow breath. "Vinnie

Despuchi is my uncle. He only gave you a job at Blackie's because I asked him to."

"Why, that's ridiculous," Sam sputtered. "I practically saved the man's life. If I hadn't picked him up in the motorhome, he might still be standing there on the side of the road."

"He was in California on business," Valerie said. "He came by the bungalow just as you were leaving, and that's when I asked him to give you a job. He didn't even know who you were. I didn't want it to look obvious, so I had him follow your little motor house. The idea was that once you got to Las Vegas, he'd introduce himself and offer you a job." She laughed suddenly. "Then you decided to go camping in the middle of the boonies, and he had to spend the night sleeping in his car. He was afraid of what you might do next, so he took a chance that you'd pick him up if he was hitchhiking."

"But why?" Sam asked. "I mean, why did you want him to give me a job? I was doing okay."

"Why? So I'd know where you were and could see you again," she cried. "Don't you understand, you big lug? I'm in love with you."

"I didn't know. I mean, I thought I knew, but I wasn't sure. I mean, I thought I was sure, but I didn't—"

"I've been in love with you for years, and when I saw you again at the Fish House, I knew I had to do something or I was going to lose you forever."

"Honest?" Sam swallowed.

"Well, not quite." Her hands went to her hair and off came the pigtails. Valerie's beautiful blonde hair cascaded down her face again. Her hands went back up and off came the beautiful blonde tresses. Now her hair was jet black, and her crystal blue eyes were the size of silver dollars.

"Virginia?" he whispered. "Virginia Beaumont?"

"Yes, Sam," she nodded slowly.

"I don't understand. Why did you change your name? And why have you been wearing a disguise?"

"The same reason you did. I just wanted to be someone else for awhile. And by the time I got my life straightened out again I was already used to what I looked like now."

Sam chuckled. "So that's why you dressed Buck up in drag. You were just trying to get even with him, you rascal."

"Oh, I'm the rascal, huh? What about you? I'm not the one who went to bed with Gilda and Tina!"

"I never laid a hand on either one of them!" Sam cried.

"It's okay, Sam. I forgive you. I just hope you can find it in your heart to forgive me. I can't lie to you anymore, and I don't want it to end like this."

End? What was she talking about? "Valerie ... uh, Virginia ... it's not going to end. It'll never end, I promise."

Then she was in his arms, crying softly, hugging him tightly. He brushed her tears away and looked into her eyes. They were like deep shady pools of water, which he could swim in forever. "Want to go to town?" he asked her softly.

"Sure, Sam," she smiled, unbuttoning her gingham dress.

"I mean, to Las Vegas! I'm starved."

She smiled lazily, then brushed her fingers across his lips. "I love you, Sam."

Sam swallowed. "Virginia, I never thought I'd say this to anyone again, but it really isn't that difficult when you find the right person. I love—"

Blam!

Blam!

Blam!

"Aw, shit," Sam exclaimed. "Who the hell could that be at this hour of the night?"

Virginia looked at her watch. "Sam, it's nine-thirty in the morning."

"Damn it, I've gotta get me a wristwatch."

"Hi, Sam," Tina said, bounding up the steps. Then she saw Virginia. "Oh! Hello."

"Don't mind her," Sam said. "It's just Valerie without her makeup on."

"My real name's Virginia. And I'm sorry if I tricked you into thinking I was somebody I wasn't. I'll never do it again."

"Oh, it's okay," Tina said nonchalantly. "It's just that I kind of got used to how you used to look, and now I've got to get used to *you*."

"So where've you been, girl?" Sam asked, pouring Tina a cup of coffee.

"I fell asleep as soon as I got to the room, and I just woke up about half an hour ago. But what I want to know is who won the poker tournament? And where the heck is Buck?"

Virginia laughed. "You tell her, Sam. I'm going to run to the grocery store and pick up some food. Can I have some money?"

"Sure," Sam said. "There's some in the medicine cabinet. And under the sink. And inside the pillow cases."

• • •

Beneath swaying palm trees, pastel casitas dotted the shoreline of Acapulco Bay. A silver jet emerged from the clouds, then slowly descended toward the airport. Inside the plane, Buck yawned and rubbed his face. Shit, his whiskers were growing out. It was a good thing Sam packed a razor in the attaché case, or Buck would be up that familiar creek again.

The plane hit the runway with a bump then squealed to a stop near a small terminal. Pancho stood and walked slowly toward the back of the cabin. "*Donde va, Ponchie?*" Buck asked, reaching for the attaché case.

"*Los velices,*" he said, turning toward Buck. "How you say, the soots in the cases?"

The velvet curtains inched open and two webbed chicken hands quickly shoved out the suitcases. Pancho scratched his head. "*Aye, caramba, Becky! Los velices deberan tener patitas porque esta ban detras de las cortinas cuando el avión partio!*" He hoisted the suitcases and trudged toward the door. "*Andalé, Ottie. Abierto, por favor.*"

The door opened and the steps unfolded. Buck picked up the attaché case. With a sigh, he followed Pancho off the plane.

Louie yanked apart the velvet curtains. "Come on, Stitch. We gotta move fast."

The two tiptoed to the door and looked out. The plane's engine had stopped. The pilot was walking toward the terminal. The Mexican man and the tall woman were at the bottom of the ladder. The man was holding two suitcases and the woman was carrying the black attaché case.

"All right, let's go over it again," Louie whispered. "You come up on the left and bump the Mexican guy. That'll get their attention. Then I come up from the other side and grab the money. Then we run through the gate and into those trees across the road. They'll never find us in there. Then we spend the rest of our lives with señoritas and margaritas. Are you ready?"

"Okay," Stitch breathed. "On twelve. One—two—three—"

"Oh, the hell with it. Let's go!"

· · ·

Buck's yellow Cadillac convertible was gone when Virginia got back to the motorhome. Sam was at the dining table, writing figures on a sheet of paper.

"Hi, honey," she said, coming through the door with an armload of groceries. "Whatcha doing?"

"Hey, this must be serious," Sam grinned, looking up. "That's the first time you ever called me honey."

"Rhymes with money," she smiled, setting the sacks down on the kitchen counter. "Where'd Tina go?"

"She's gone to pay off Buck's markers, then she's gonna contact all the people in the show and tell them to get their money from Larry Noble." Leaning back in his chair, Sam laughed. "God, I'd love to see old Larry's face when fifty-eight singers and dancers and trapeze artists all show up at his office at the same time with their hands out."

"Is she going back to California?"

"I talked her out of it. I think she's got a great future right here at Blackie's."

"So what are you doing now?" Virginia asked, putting groceries away.

"I was just figuring out how much dough we've got left. Counting the half-million from the poker tournament, we've got a grand total of—five hundred two thousand four hundred and fifty-eight dollars. And that's after giving twenty-five thousand to Buck!"

"Gosh, honey, that's great."

"And tomorrow I'm going to give Uncle Vinnie his half-million. Then you and I will take over Blackie's. You'll never serve another cocktail again."

Virginia opened the oven door, then pulled out a wrinkled stack of ten dollar bills. "Better add this to your inventory," she smiled, tossing the money to Sam, then lighting the pilot light.

Sam spread the money out and started counting again. "I'm thinking about adding a room on the motorhome," he said. "As rich as we are, we should have a live-in maid."

"Are you getting hungry?" Virginia asked, getting two plates out of the cabinet and tossing another stack of bills to Sam.

"Yeah, I'm famished. What are we having, anyway?"

"Roast turkey, dressing, mashed potatoes and gravy, green beans with almonds, candied yams, cranberry sauce, hot biscuits, tossed salad, and homemade chocolate cake with ice cream."

"What's the big occasion?"

"Today's my birthday."

"Your birthday?" Sam cried. "Why didn't you say something? I would have got you something nice." He stood and took her in his arms. "Something really nice—like a wedding ring."

"Oh, Sam, I love you."

"How old are you anyway?"

"Twenty-one."

Sam's stomach somersaulted skyward.

. . .

Three months later, two musicians stood on a street corner in Acapulco. As they sang and strummed their homemade guitars, they stared solemnly at the cup near their feet. On the cup was written the word TIPS, but the cup was empty.

"Chicken wings, and a bottle of gin
Chicken wings, and a bottle of gin
Chicken wings, and a bottle of gin
We're gonna have ourselves some fun tonight ..."

One of the musicians wore a brown and orange shirt with little silver corner pieces on the collar tips, a tattered tan coat with curly brown embroidery, and the bottom half of a chicken outfit. The other wore the top half of an alligator costume, torn tan slacks with curly brown embroidery, and a scuffed pair of boots that were obviously too large for his feet.

Behind the musicians a line of people waited outside a movie theater. The marquee advertised the night's movie in bold black letters.

PANCHO MORALES PRESENTE
BECKY SUNNYBROOK EN
"LA SEÑORITA AMERICANA"

. . .

In Las Vegas, the ballroom of Blackie's Casino was crowded with employees. Behind a podium stood Vinnie Despuchi, dressed in a black suit, black shirt, and white tie.

"I want to thank everyone for being here," he said into the microphone. "You've all been reading the newspapers, so you know the casino has been sold. Today it's my great pleasure to introduce the new owner—Samuel Duran!"

Sam stood to a smattering of applause. "Samuel?" he whispered to Vinnie.

"Yeah," Vinnie grunted. "Sounds more dignified."

Sam cleared his throat and looked out at the assemblage of cocktail waitresses, dealers, security guards, cashiers, and all the others who made up a casino operation.

"The first one of you who calls me Samuel goes on graveyard shift." A few chuckles. "You might remember me as a dealer here, so if I can run a casino, anybody can. In fact, I've got a few promotions to announce today." Sam turned and gestured to a group of people seated on stage. "Ron Hartley is our new security chief. Shorty, Tiny, and Pee Wee have retired, and are being replaced as pit bosses by Vito, Carlo, and Gino. Our new entertainment director is Tina Forlorne. And the number-two man at Blackie's from now on is my wife Virginia." Polite applause.

"I want you to know your jobs at Blackie's are secure, and that the door to my office will always be open." Nothing.

"And starting today, each employee at Blackie's is getting a raise of ten dollars a day." Thunderous applause.

"Eight paid holidays a year." More thunderous applause.

"A retirement plan for all employees, with the company matching your contribution." Deafening applause.

"And next week we start construction on a new tower that will double the number of rooms in our hotel." The applause began to die down.

"So what do you say we just close up for the weekend—with pay, of course—and I'll see you all here on Monday. Thank you."

Suddenly all the employees surged toward Sam, and for a fleeting moment he found himself reaching for his trusty six-shooter. Then he was on somebody's shoulders and being paraded through the casino. He caught sight of Virginia and shrugged helplessly.

"I love you," she mouthed to him.

"I LOVE YOU!" he shouted.

"WE LOVE YOU, TOO!" the employees shouted.

And that's how Blackie's, later to be known as Virginia City, became the most successful casino operation in the history of Las Vegas.

About the Author

Barney Vinson was born in the U.S.A., raised in Texas, and moved to Las Vegas a long time ago. He worked as a dice dealer at the old Dunes Hotel, then went to Caesars Palace where he was the casino gaming instructor for another long time. He lives in a small house by the side of the road with the Vegas skyline in the distance and writes full-time, while his wife Debbie works and pays the bills; they take in stray cats by appointment only. Vinson is the author of 23 books (six of which have been published); *The Vegas Kid* is his first novel.

About Huntington Press

Huntington Press is a specialty publisher of Las Vegas-and gambling-related books and periodicals. To receive a copy of the Huntington Press catalog, call 1-800-244-2224 or write to the address below.

Huntington Press
3687 South Procyon Avenue
Las Vegas, Nevada 89103
E-mail: books@huntingtonpress.com